CORNERED!

Wild Bill looked calm enough, as he always did except when trapped by Calamity Jane. But Josh read trouble in his eyes, even a glint of uncertainty.

"Cover me from the corner of the house, kid," Bill said, still watching the street for trouble. "That back right corner, where the willow tree will give you good cover."

Josh eased out his old French pinfire and cocked it. Both men slipped into the shadowy side yard of Ma's Bunkhouse.

"Listen up, kid," Bill whispered. "This ain't Miles City, *don't* go for glory. No matter what happens to me, don't be a fool and go beyond that corner, hear? They'll cut you down faster than a finger snap."

Josh swallowed the lump in his throat. "You kidding? Don't worry, I've seen what these two can do, remember?"

"But then again, if you get a good bead on one of 'em," Bill added, "drill the son-of-a-bitch."

WILD BILL

JUDD COLE

BLEEDING KANSAS

LEISURE BOOKS NEW YORK CITY

A LEISURE BOOK®

September 1999

Published by

Dorchester Publishing Co., Inc.
276 Fifth Avenue
New York, NY 10001

ISBN 0-8439-4584-2

BLEEDING KANSAS

Chapter One

"Raise you two bits, Wild Bill," said a thin man wearing clergy black. His watery nose made him sniff a lot.

"Give as good as you get," James Butler Hickok replied amiably.

He poked his cheroot between his teeth and flipped fifty cents into the pot. "See you, old son, and raise you another two bits."

The dealer, nineteen-year-old Joshua Robinson, goggled at the pot heaped up on the green baize surface of the poker table. Almost twenty dollars and still growing!

"Better slow down, Pretty Bill," warned a striking redhead wearing a low-cut dress with velvet-trimmed cuffs. She crowded Bill's right elbow. "You've lost the last three hands; soon you won't have two nickels left to rub together. You can't take me to Paris if you're broke!"

"You go right ahead and lose your money, Billy," chimed in a swollen-bodiced blonde crowding his left elbow. "I've got savings, I'll take *you* to Paris, you handsome lug."

Josh felt a sting of jealousy. These gals were not your typical soiled doves who entertained cowboys in seedy cribs behind the saloon. These were respectable dime-a-dance girls.

In fact, Josh had struck a spark for the sweet little redhead less than an hour after he and Wild Bill rode into Miles City, Montana. Yet, respectable or not, she soon made it quite clear she'd gladly trade her favors for a night of unbridled lust with the hero of *Wild Bill the Indian Slayer*.

"Bill won't need money in Paris, sweet love," said another gambler at the table, a neat young hardware drummer in a high, brightly glazed paper collar. His straw sample case leaned against his leg. "He's famous in France, too. So *I'll* take this pot."

He laid down an ace-high straight and scooped in his winnings.

"Famous men *still* have to pay their hotel bills," Wild Bill carped good-naturedly. "Ante up, gents! I won't leave this table until I'm a rich man or a pauper. Deal, kid, and cowards to the rear!"

Josh shuffled the cards, watching the redhead nibble Bill's ear while the busty blonde topped off his pony glass with Old Taylor bourbon.

He never gets woman-hungry like the rest of us, Josh realized in another flush of resentment. *That's* why the females flock to him like flies to syrup. It's not just his fame—men who were indifferent to women got their pick of the feminine litter.

"Looks like we have company, gents," said the fourth player at the table, an Army officer with his tunic unbuttoned. He nodded toward the front of the building.

Word had quickly gotten noised about that Wild Bill Hickok was in town. By now the town loafers had congregated outside, gawking above the bat wings like chawbacons at a county fair.

"They all wanna touch you for luck, hon," the blonde said to Hickok. "Everybody knows how often the Rebels captured you and sentenced you to death, you slippery devil."

Josh saw one of her slim hands disappear under the table. "We *all* like to touch you," she added.

"Careful there, dumpling," Bill warned her. "You break it; you pay for it."

"I told you I got savings," she reminded him shamelessly. Josh flushed and glanced away, glad his mother didn't realize the kind of women he had fallen among.

The Songbird Saloon was typical of dozens of watering holes Josh and Bill had frequented since Josh came west in search of a living American legend named Hickok. Tin lamp reflectors lined the walls. There were brass cuspidors scattered about, but the condition of the rough floor planks proved few ever hit them. A sign on the nearest wall warned: NO ROADHOUSE TALK ON SUN-DAYS, GODDAMNIT!

It was early autumn, the nights up north were starting to get a snap to them and left a thin powdering of frost on the grass at sunup. A rusty stove sat on bricks and emitted a ruby flush from coals glowing in the firebox. In the corner nearest the stove huddled the local old-timers who had retired to the liar's nook. They played checkers and nine men's morris, ignoring the young bucks with open contempt.

"Sheep clouds making up," Josh heard one of them remark. "We'll have rain in twenty-four hours, I expect."

The poker game went forward, coins clinking, cards slapping the table. Outside, a fierce wind polished the knolls bare and made the saloon's joists groan in protest. Once again Josh felt it: that prickling of the nape, that tingle along his spine. Danger lurked very nearby; Josh could feel its presence like a hand on his shoulder.

The youth recalled riding into Miles City and Wild Bill's comment. How this burg put him in mind of the mining camps in the Black Hills—places, Bill insisted, that surpassed even Tombstone, Arizona, for sheer violence.

Even now, despite clearly enjoying the game, Wild Bill displayed his habitual vigilance. He sat with his back to the wall, commanding a good view of the entire room. There was a filthy back-bar mirror, and Josh saw Bill using it to good advantage. Though his long gray duster hid them, two ivory-handled Colt Peacemakers were only inches from Hickok's fabled hands.

The short-line stage rolled through town, tug chains rattling. Hearing it, Wild Bill looked at Josh and said quietly, "C. J."

Josh nodded, put down the deck of cards, and walked outside to quickly check the streets. He watched a woman with a small child emerge from the stage and hustle into the town's only hotel. A sudden wind gust made Josh shiver in his summer-weight suit. Soon enough, snow water would fill the ruts of these streets, glazing over with ice after sunset. Josh pictured all this soft mud after bitter-cold winds turned it hard as baked adobe.

A wedge of geese passed overhead, winging south. They made a racket like a pack of hounds. Josh shivered at the lonely sound, again thinking how close danger felt.

He returned to the table.

"All clear," he told Bill, dealing out the next hand.

"Who in Sam Hill is C. J.?" the blonde demanded. "I thought this little clerk's name was Joshua."

Josh felt heat flooding his cheeks.

"I ain't no damned clerk," he protested. "I'm a newspaper writer. And for the *New York Herald*, the country's greatest newspaper."

11

The buxom femme snorted. "The 'Noo Yawk Cat's Tail,' you mean! Newspaper writer! Huh! Little old ladies of both sexes."

Josh was steamed but continued to deal cards with a stoic face. A faint crease in Wild Bill's forehead told Josh that his hero was laughing hard inside at him. Like an Indian at a treaty ceremony, Bill had perfected the silent "abdomen laugh."

"What brings you to Montana, Wild Bill?" remarked the Army officer, who was quite civil to all despite an indrawn, bitter look Josh had spotted often on career soldiers along the frontier.

"Oh, a mere trifle, Soldier Blue. I and Longfellow here had a little business with an extortion gang operating up near Lewistown," Bill replied. "These were some rough, unshaven fellows with poor manners. Figured they could exact tribute from cattlemen."

The skinny man in clerical black chuckled. "I'd wager those 'rough, unshaven fellows' have found a new line of work, anh?"

"The ones that can still shave," Bill conceded amiably, "have taken a sudden interest in the Canadian Rockies. Good bass fishing up that way, I'm told."

"Just like you done with the McCanles gang, right, Bill?" the blonde fawned.

Josh frowned petulantly when she added, taking her "facts" straight from the dime novels and shilling shockers, "Wild Bill wiped out ten members of the gang at Rock Creek, Nebraska."

"Six with his guns," chimed in the redhead, "and four with the bowie knife he always keeps tucked in his red sash."

"*What* bowie knife?" Josh protested. "*What* red—"

"I'll take two, kid," Bill cut in. "And didn't that Quaker mama of yours in Philly teach you never to talk over a lady? Shame, boy, shame!"

Josh slapped the cards down like he was smashing bugs. Man alive! In truth, Bill only killed two of the McCanles bunch and wounded a third. But Josh noticed how Wild Bill never made any effort whatsoever to deny the melodramatic claims of ink-slinging hacks. Bill didn't lie himself; he just never corrected the record.

One of the wall lamps began to gutter. The barkeep cut a new wick from his long johns and soon had it fixed.

A conveyance rattled into town. Bill looked at Josh. "C. J."

The youth dutifully rose, went outside to check on the new arrival, came back inside.

"All clear," Josh reported as he resumed dealing. "Just a farmer in a manure wagon. I saw a messenger boy coming from the telegraph office."

"Good," Bill said. "Must be for me. 'Bout damn time Pinkerton wired us."

13

"Who's this C. J. you're watching for?" the red-head demanded.

"Christ Jesus," Bill said with a straight face. "He's due back any day now."

"Mr. Hickok," said the young drummer as he sorted his cards, "I read the fascinating interview you gave to *Harper's Weekly*. I recall one line especially: 'The West can be harsh, but most men mean no harm!' Hear, hear!"

"An interesting and generous sentiment," the officer added, "coming from a man who's become the most sought-after target in the West."

The bat wings slapped open. Josh and Wild Bill both glanced up in the dimness and spotted the official red livery of a Western Union boy. Hickok's famous hair-trigger alertness relaxed a bit.

But say, Josh thought, peering closer. *That's* not the same kid I just spotted! That's—

Later, Josh realized how all of it happened as quick as a heartbeat. Even as Bill opened his mouth to reply to the officer, a blue-tinted Colt .44 appeared in the fist of the approaching figure, now about ten paces from the table.

"Well, God kiss me!" Wild Bill said in pure astonishment at being tricked. He used both arms to shove the two women out of harm's way. That delay was fatal—the Colt was aimed dead at Hickok's lights, and the gunman already taking up his trigger slack.

14

The detonation of gunpowder was deafening in that low-ceilinged room. One of the women screamed; the soldier dove to the floor. A second later, the only sound was the obscene, liquid slapping of blood spurting to the floor.

The blonde moaned once, then swooned into the drummer's arms.

The redhead stared at Josh. He still held his pinfire revolver in his right fist, smoke curling from the muzzle. The gunman lay sprawled in his own blood. A foot twitched, and with no hesitation Wild Bill tossed a finishing shot into the downed man. Hickok feared possum players from his war days.

"The boy killed him!" marveled the redhead. "He saved Wild Bill Hickok's bacon! Bill froze right up, and the kid—"

"Now ease off that 'froze up' crap," Bill protested. "There were ladies in the line of fire, I had to—"

"*Never* talk over a lady," Josh reminded the living legend. "Shame on you, Wild Bill, shame."

"The kid—Joshua, I mean—drew that weapon so fast," the redhead praised. She scooted her chair closer to his.

"And plugged the bastard dead center," the soldier added after examining the body.

"*I* taught that kid how to shoot," Hickok said defensively. "I gave him that gun! Hell, this little city slick didn't even know factory ammo from

15

hand crimped."

"Well, he was an apt pupil," said the drummer, beaming at Josh. "This lad's a hero, Bill! Saved your life, for a surety!"

"Wasn't for him," the soldier agreed, "Bill'd be looking up to see daisies."

" 'Preciate it, kid," Bill said in a flat tone.

The redhead began flirting with Josh. The youth saw something truly rare flicker in Hickok's gun-metal eyes: jealousy!

"At least reach me that telegram, wouldja, kid?" Wild Bill groused. "I hope it's orders from Pinkerton. I'm sick of this one-horse town."

Josh grinned ear-to-ear as he pulled the yellow message form from the dead man's grip. But he read the telegram before he handed it to Hickok.

Like a snow flake melting on a river, the grin disappeared from Josh's face.

Chapter Two

"Well, I wanted orders from Pinkerton," Hickok admitted after he and Josh returned to the hotel. "Now that I've got my damned orders, I'm half a mind to quit working for that old miser. Damn him to hell, anyway. Any town but that one."

Josh watched Bill palm the wheel of one of his Colts, checking his loads. He had already thumbed home a cartridge to replace the one he spent at the Songbird.

The telegram sat atop a little escritoire beside Josh's narrow, iron bedstead. The young reporter's latest dispatch sat beside it, awaiting release over the newly formed wires of the Associated Press. Josh watched Bill idly run a finger over his neat blond mustache as he gazed at the telegraph, an odd glint in his eyes.

"Any damn place on earth but that one," Bill repeated, sliding his Colt back into its hand-tooled holster. "Send me to Cochise County, Arizona, hell, I won't whimper. Send me up to the Comstock, make me ride shotgun on a bullion coach in the ass end of west Texas, I'm your boy. But Abilene, Kansas? Old son, that's too much hell for one sinner."

Bill cursed softly and slid a cheroot from his vest, skinning back the wrapper. Footsteps sounded out in the carpeted hall, and Bill focused his attention out there until they passed.

As for Josh, he was nervously pacing the small room. He'd read once that cowboys on long roundups became restless inside buildings, and Josh felt that cooped-up restlessness himself now in his hotel room.

"Take it easy, kid," Bill said absent-mindedly, as if he were speaking to calm a nerved-up horse. "It's your first kill. You'll be off your feed for a couple days, miss some sleep. It'll pass. You done good, that jasper needed killing."

Bill scratched a phosphor with his thumbnail and puffed the cigar to life. Despite his words just now, he still watched the kid from a sullen deadpan.

Still mad at me, Josh thought. He's a prideful man, and I made him look bad in front of others. Josh was feeling less brash now that the reality of killing a man—even one as low as that murdering trash in the saloon—was setting in.

Besides, Josh realized, Wild Bill really did make a gallant choice in pushing those two sparkling doxies out of harm's way rather than drawing his weapon.

But Hickok, never a man to hold a grudge, was seeing some humor in all of it, too. Now he cocked his head and watched Josh, a grudging little grin tugging at his thin lips.

"The cat sits by the gopher hole, right, Longfellow? Just bides his time. Waits for the perfect moment to pounce, anh?"

"Whad 'ya mean?"

"Never mind, you crafty little devil! That redhead will eat you alive and spit out your bones! We got us a tougher nut to crack, old son."

Bill nodded toward the telegram. Josh picked it up and read it once again:

JAMIE: SNIPER TERRORIZING ABILENE. I CAN'T ORDER YOU BACK TO THAT HELLHOLE. BUT THIS REQUIRES MY BEST OP, AND THAT'S YOU. SITUATION URGENT. REPLY IMMEDIATELY. ALLAN

"You taking the job?" Josh demanded.

For a moment Hickok's face got a tight-to-the-bone look on it, one Josh recognized well since coming west. Very few men out here ever saved money, including Bill Hickok. They lived high while they were solvent, sought work when their pockets were empty.

"Damnit, kid, I have to. I'm in a dirty corner, and poker won't get me out of it. But why Abilene? Of all the little stage-stop hellholes in Kansas, why *that* one? I cleaned it up once already and damn near caught a load of lead whistlers for my trouble. I figure it's somebody else's turn to skin that grizzly."

But something else was rankling in Bill's craw, and Josh saw him stare at the telegram again.

"The sheriff," Bill mused, unaware his cigar had gone cold, "says he found the real Western Union boy in an alley, conked on the cabeza. Now, ain't that a mite queer?"

Josh replied slowly, thinking it out: "You mean . . . how the killer would know there was a telegram coming for you?"

Wild Bill nodded; his gunmetal eyes narrowed as he worked this trail out. "At first I figured it was just another try at collecting the open reward on my head."

Bill meant the open bounty of $10,000 that had been placed on him when he served as sheriff of Abilene. He had been forced to shoot a drunk, kill-crazy cowboy named Harlan Lofley. But Lofley's old man was one of the richest cattlemen in Texas, and the doting old patriarch wanted his son's killer planted.

"But if it was just a reward seeker," Bill added, "why the link to this telegram?"

"You mean," Josh said, his reporter's nose starting to sniff a story here, "that somebody's been *waiting* for Pinkerton to telegraph you? Somebody within Western Union?"

Bill nodded. "Somebody who expects me to be sent to Abilene. Whatever's going on down there, it must be some pumpkins if security is this tight. Hand me that nib and ink, wouldja?"

Josh watched Bill dip a brass nib into a little pot of ink, then scratch out a short message on a sheet of hotel stationery.

"We'll get more information from Pinkerton," Bill said, handing the sheet to Josh. "But take this to the telegraph office and wire it to him immediately. We need to make sure all future communications are secure."

Josh read the brief message: " 'Telegraph may be compromised. Use the code.' What code?"

"Me and Pinkerton used it when we worked together during the war," Bill explained. "It's called an alphanumeric code; you can change it at any time. Each letter of the alphabet gets a numerical value that stands for a completely different letter. Say, the letter *A* equals five or the fifth letter of the alphabet. It's cumbersome but safe."

"Man alive! Espionage! But shouldn't this be in code, too?"

Bill shook his head. "Nope. Cuz I want you to study the telegrapher's face close for me, Longfellow, use all that writer's intuition. Watch him close while he's tapping out the Morse, decide what you think about him."

Josh was halfway to the door when Bill added, "Kid?"

He turned around. "Yeah?"

"C. J. Keep a weather eye out for her."

Josh paled a little. "You still think she's looking for you?"

Bill nodded. "No bout adoubt it."

He added a sly grin as he relit his cheroot. "And if she can't find me, young Joshua, *you'll* do just fine."

"Brother," complained Ansel Logan, "why don't God at least send me a woman out here?"

"Your trouble," said his huge companion in a lazy southern drawl, "is that you always want toast 'steada bread. The hell's your dicker, anyhow? You sit on your duff all day for top dollar. *I* do all the work."

'Bama Jones said all this while he carefully cleared stones and debris aside, leveling off a spot to set up a metal bipod. The two men occupied a stand of scrub pine, a rare island in a sea of grass in central Kansas just west of the sprawling stockyards at Abilene.

"Work?" repeated Logan, mocking the word. "Look who's feelin' a mite scratchy today. You don't know what you're talkin' about when it comes to work, you tub of lard. Nobody shoots back at you."

"That's on account I always kill what I aim at."

"You sayin' I don't?"

"Ahh, go crap in your hat."

'Bama grunted hard when he dropped to his knees beside the bipod. He wore filthy buckskin trousers, a faded gray Rebel tunic, a broad-brimmed plainsman's hat. The tunic no longer fit, and he'd left the buttons unlooped.

Logan watched him, picking his teeth with a twig. His companion opened a buckskin rifle sheath. With loving care, 'Bama removed a Big Fifty Sharps equipped with a fancy German scope. The weapon fired 700-grain slugs that could easily drop an adult buffalo from a mile off.

Logan rolled a smoke and expertly quirled both ends. He was short, but descended from big-boned Ulster stock, the same tough, hard-knit men who filled the ranks of America's police forces and Army barracks. He wore fancy star-roweled spurs of Mexican silver. His steel-framed Smith & Wesson pistol was tied low on his thigh. He had filed off the notch on the hammer so it wouldn't snag coming out of the holster.

Logan raised a pair of brass field glasses and turned his stubbled profile to the north, studying the distant activity along the horizon. He spotted a team of work mules, their bits flecked with foam.

"I see plenty of targets," he announced with satisfaction. Everything in his face smiled except the eyes. "They got a surveyor and an assistant holding the sticks for him. Plus you got free pick from the grading crew."

"Like shootin' fish in a barrel," 'Bama agreed, taking up a prone position behind the Big Fifty, now secured to the bipod. "It's no skin off my ass which one I drop."

"Air out the surveyor," Logan suggested. "They're worth more."

"Out here *I* run the roost," 'Bama reminded him. "And I don't take guff from you. I pick the targets."

"Don't get your bowels in an uproar, porky. I'm just tryin' to help."

"*Help* yourself straight to hell."

'Bama wisely bit back a harsher reply. Ansel Logan, he had learned from experience, was a bomb with a very short fuse. Like a wild Indian, he was capable of instant brutality at any moment. And the former circus shootist had few, if any, peers when it came to drawing and shooting a short iron. That's why Logan had been hired as 'Bama's personal bodyguard for this job. As 'Bama had insisted to the railroad baron who secretly hired him—he was a sniper, not a gunfighter.

"Reach me them spy glasses," 'Bama said.

The big man pushed his hat back, then studied the Kansas-Pacific work crew.

A scout had passed by earlier. But 'Bama let him go when he saw the man's brass stirrups— former Reb cavalry. This surveyor below was a thin, hatless man with a soup-strainer mustache. He was just now stretching out a Gunter's chain, sighting through the route for a new spur line. Behind him, the graders leveled off a low ridge, preparing the way for the track layers.

'Bama chuckled, tickling his trigger. "Oh, Chumley! This is like money for old rope. Get set to hightail it."

'Bama centered the crosshair sight just above the surveyor's left ear.

"Gotta drop two clicks for elevation," he muttered to himself, whispering like a man in church. "And add one click right for windage."

"How's 'at?" Logan said. "Speak up!"

"Shh," 'Bama whispered. "Shush it now, bo. It's time to kiss the mistress."

An eerie, intense focus came over the big sniper's moon face. Damn, Logan thought, feeling his skin prickle. That son of a bitch looks like he's taking a woman.

'Bama inhaled a long breath, expelled it slowly while he relaxed his entire body. His trigger finger took up the slack in one long, continuous pull.

"Shh," he said with gentle reverence. "Shhh! Just a little-bitty kiss. . . . "

Logan, watching through the glasses, flinched hard when the Big Fifty suddenly exploded. The top of the surveyor's head lifted off as neatly as

25

the lid of a cookie jar, releasing a pebbly spray of blood and brains.

The surveyor's knees buckled like an empty sack, and the body folded into a twitching heap.

"Hellfire!" Logan roared. "You may smell like a bear's cave, 'Bama. But gawd*damn* can you aim a smoke pole!"

'Bama whooped and shook a fist as solid as a cedar mallet. "Hell, I ain't had this much fun since the hogs ate Maw-maw!"

"Let's make tracks," Logan urged. "They're pointing over this way."

A sorrel and a claybank—good horseflesh, but both badly neglected—waited for them in a nearby defile, hobbled foreleg to rear. By the time the shaken pursuers had saddled mounts to give chase, the long-distance killing team had opened up an insurmountable lead.

Chapter Three

" 'Killed instantly,' " Josh read out loud from the Ellsworth, Kansas, *Advocate*, " 'was Danny O'Neil, 34, a chief surveyor who had worked for the Kansas-Pacific Railroad since August 1865. As with the other killings recently plaguing the Kansas Pacific, the assassin used a high-powered rifle from a tremendous distance. Witnesses estimate the killer fired from almost a mile away, This—' "

"Whoa there," Wild Bill cut in. He snapped his head around from the monotonous view out the train window to stare at his young companion. "Did you skip a line? A *mile* away?"

"A mile, yessir. It's got to be the sniper Pinkerton mentioned."

"The way you say," Bill agreed.

"And since the sniper is killing so many KP workers," Josh continued, building a case like a lawyer, "doesn't that point to a competing railroad line?"

"A good bet, but not a sure one. They call it railroad law out here, and it does get mean. But could also be a wealthy cattleman behind it. There's three cattle trails coming out of Texas, and each one ends at a different railhead. This new spur line the KP is building will draw even more of the cattle business to Abilene. There's others would love to see it swing south to Dodge City or Newton."

Wild Bill fell silent, turning his face to the window again. Outside, the vast Great Plains rolled on toward the unbroken horizon. Country so wide open, Josh had written in a recent dispatch, a man could almost see tomorrow.

"Almost a mile away," Bill muttered thoughtfully. Josh watched him frown so deeply that his reddish-blond eyebrows nearly met.

The two friends had almost an entire Pullman luxury car to themselves. Green plush leather, satin curtains, new gas lights, even a piano for sing-alongs. The Kansas-Pacific had booked special passage for both men and their horses. It wasn't just Hickok's fabled reputation—the famous frontiersman was a former railroad scout and guard who had saved plenty of lives at great risk. Now he rode free everywhere on any line in America, even back east.

But in remote Miles City, the two men had to board a no-frills, narrow-gauge mining train financed by private investors. It brought them down from the Yellowstone drainage, following the Powder River south. West of Fort Laramie, in the Wyoming Territory, they transferred to the Union Pacific line for the long, serpentine journey through the North Platte and South Platte valleys.

At Ogallala, Nebraska, they jogged due south on horseback to connect with the KP at a remote water stop. Now they were only a few hours west of Abilene.

After a minute of mulling things, Josh spoke up.

"That 'mile,' " he suggested, "could be a stretch. Most newspaper writers don't know beans from buckshot about marksmanship."

Josh hadn't meant to sound like he was boasting. But Hickok snorted. "They ain't been to high school in Philadelphia like you have," Bill roweled the kid.

But Hickok added, "There's at least one man I know of who can kill at a mile. But I figured him for dead by now. Hoped so, anyhow."

"Who?" Josh demanded.

Wild Bill, Josh had learned long ago, had an aggravating habit of ignoring questions until he was good and ready to answer them. He did so now, chewing thoughtfully on an unlit cigar.

"Pinkerton," Bill said, "is sending more information by special courier from Denver. But I like your theory, kid, about railroad competition. I've heard some scuttlebutt about how the Santa Fe Railroad is looking to push a line through southern Kansas. If they could stop this new KP line cold, or even slow it down considerable, that's money in the bank for them."

The door at the end of the corridor swung open, and Hickok automatically scrutinized the new arrival. It was a porter with a wooden bucket. He filled it from the Pullman's ice closet and left again. Perhaps recalling the "delivery boy" in Miles City, Hickok kept the porter in constant sight until he was gone.

Bill noticably relaxed again. This kind of routine vigilance was required night and day, Josh realized. So many sensation-seeking hack writers pretended it was such great larks to be the most sought-after target on the lawless frontier. But his few short months at Bill's side had convinced Josh that "excitement" was for clerks and old ladies—a man gets damned tired, damned quick, of constantly looking over his shoulder. And now look! Hickok was returning, of all places, to Abilene. Not just the lion's den, for him, but the lion's jaws.

"Bill?"

"Mmm?"

"Who's this man you say can kill from a mile off?"

But again Bill frowned and ignored the meat of the question.

"Out here," Hickok mused, "the outlaw trail is long and crowded. The war made plenty of new criminals from both sides. And plenty of them have drifted west on the dodge. Could be anybody. Anybody, kid. This is Bleeding Kansas."

Josh nodded. He knew that Jayhawkers still plagued the new state. Abolitionist guerrillas during the war, they were now just plundering, murdering thieves. There were also the so-called holdout Rebels who once rode under insane marauders like Quantrille.

Bill shifted his shell belt, transferring its considerable weight so it could chafe a new spot.

"Well, Longfellow," he remarked, "you told that Quaker ma of yours yet?"

"Told her what?"

Bill gave another little fluming snort like a horse drinking. "Ain't *he* the frosty one! 'Told her what?' Told her that her son has killed a man, that's what."

Now it was Josh who sought refuge in the view outside. "Naw. It wouldn't set too well with her. She made me promise to turn the other cheek."

"That sweet-lavender humility is all right for some. I like a gentle, peace-loving man, matter fact. But I'm damn glad you got starch in your collar, kid. You kept me above the ground a bit longer. You'll do to take along."

"Thanks. Hey, Bill?"

"Hey what?"

"You *do* know who this sniper is, don'tcha?"

"Yeah," Bill confirmed. " 'Fraid I do. But I won't say his name today."

"Aww, man alive, Bill! Why not?"

"Cuz," Bill replied with his usual poker face, "it's Sunday."

"So what?"

"Even a heathen like me," Bill said in a flat, humorless tone, "won't pronounce the Devil's name on the Sabbath."

Every hour or so, the two men went back to the stock car and checked on their horses.

Josh's quick little piebald, only fourteen hands but broke to halter by a Sioux warrior, acted nervous and fretful despite a roomy stall, clean straw, and the nose bags of crushed barley Josh had strapped on with generous regularity.

However, Fire-away, Wild Bill's pretty little strawberry roan, had learned long ago to enjoy train travel. The gelding greeted both men with a contented whicker, nuzzling Bill's shoulder.

"We'll stretch out the kinks at the next water stop," Bill promised his horse, scratching its withers.

Bill kicked open the sliding door to let some fresh air blow in. Josh felt autumn cold slice at his neck, and he turned up his collar. He looked out over the waving grass, stirrup-high in some places.

Bill stood quietly beside him, also looking out. But Josh got the definite impression Wild Bill was seeing only with his inner eye. His next remark confirmed this.

"Out here, no trees for hanging a man," Bill observed.

"Do they execute outlaws with bullets?"

Bill took his cigar—lit now—out of his teeth and frowned at it. "Nope. You just drag-hang 'em behind a horse is all. It's still a necktie party but with plenty of dust."

Josh wasn't sure if Bill was twitting him—with Wild Bill, it was sometimes hard to tell the line between fact and irony. The tracks dipped close to a creek, and Josh spotted a nester digging holes and setting posts. Slab lumber was rare out here. Most buildings were made of sod bricks, and most corrals of sturdy Osage orange planted close together.

They passed an Abilene-bound stagecoach rocking on its braces. The horses looked worn down from pulling mud-caked wheels. Still, Wild Bill seemed to see little of this.

It's because we're getting closer to Abilene, Josh figured. But again Bill's next question suggested otherwise.

"You're sure," he asked Josh for the second time, "everything seemed jake at the Miles City Western Union?"

"The telegrapher never batted an eye at your message. Honest Injun. I'll bet the telegraph lines are safe."

Bill shook his head. "I wouldn't put one red penny on that. He was just a good actor. Somebody *knew* we had a message coming and was waiting right there for it."

Josh started to ask once again about the mystery sniper who was troubling Bill. But an exclamation from Hickok cut him short.

"Well, God kiss me! Wouldja look at *that*, kid?"

Now Bill was indeed staring outside, and pointing, too. Josh followed his finger, then felt a jolt of shock.

"Ho-ly Hannah!" the youth exclaimed, unable to believe his eyes.

About fifty yards away, parallel with their train car, a ruggedly built Studebaker Brothers wagon bounced and jostled across the prairie at a brisk clip.

A woman—hell, thought Josh, a *girl*—was hunched over on the box, clinging for dear life while her blond braids flew out behind her like lance streamers. Three little tow-headed kids were crowded close behind her, faces drained white with fear.

But what Josh couldn't believe, despite the evidence of his senses, was the fact that no team pulled the wagon!

The wagon tongue had been tied up to keep it from dragging. And a sturdy pole—now a mast—rose from the center of the wagon bed. A huge white wagon cover, swollen tight with a stiff west wind, now served as a main sail!

34

"Great day in the morning!" Josh exclaimed. "It's a prairie schooner!"

"The wind has got too strong," Bill said. "Christ, they're going full-bore! She's going to crack up, the damned little fool!"

"Kid," he added, giving Josh a push, "climb up topside and tell the brakemen to start turning their wheels. She swerves left, we'll run right over her."

Josh hustled above while Bill watched the girl trying to slow down the flying juggernaut her wagon had become. But even as Bill watched, the wooden brake handle snapped off in her hand. The Studebaker dipped into a swale and nearly capsized.

If it goes over, it could crush those kids, Bill thought, sliding the Peacemaker from his right holster. Even as the metallic groan of braking train wheels began, Bill aimed six well-placed shots at one spot on the mast, weakening it considerably.

It snapped with a decisive crack, twisting off to one side and falling away. The sudden loss of forward power caught the girl by surprise. Even as the runaway wagon lurched slower, she went flying from the box in a forward somersault.

The train ground to a halt a few hundred yards farther on. Bill and Josh leaped down and trotted back to the disabled wagon.

Abruptly, Bill laughed so hard he had to punch his thigh.

"Jesus, Longfellow, look! She landed smack in a buffalo wallow!"

Josh goggled as the pretty blonde—a faded blue anchor-print dress clinging to her underweight frame—pulled herself out of the slimy, smelly muck.

"You looking for the Pacific Ocean, sailor?" Bill greeted her, still chuckling. "Or the Atlantic?"

"You go to hell!" she fired back, her cornflower-blue eyes smoky with anger. Josh saw now that she was definitely a woman, though hardly older than he.

"We was headed straight for Abilene until *you* stopped us, mister!" she added, glowering at Hickok.

"You leave my sister alone!" shouted a little shirttail brat who couldn't have been more than seven years old. "You damned ignorant yahoos!" the boy added defiantly, probably imitating his pa.

"Simmer down, alla you," Bill said, trying to keep a straight face. "You would've killed yourselves trying to make Abilene in *that* rig, dumpling. The hell you doing running all over Robin Hood's barn without a team?"

Josh had risked the hostile stares of the children to peek into the bed of the wagon. To his considerable surprise, the bed was crowded with seedling trees. Their roots had been packed in dirt and wrapped with layers of damp burlap.

"My name is Kristen McCoy," she informed Bill with fractured dignity, swiping gobs of mud from her dress. "The McCoys of Fort Wayne, Indiana. My father, may he rest in peace, had the finest fruit orchards in the state. We came west to file a homestead. My father intends—*intended*—to introduce the first fruit trees on the Great Plains. But he drowned when we forded the Arkansas River."

"And your ma?" Bill asked.

"She died of childbed fever after my sister Jenny was born."

Hearing all this, the mirth left Bill's face. He looked at these orphans, noticing how thin and slat-ribbed they were. The girl, too. They'd all been through some hard slogging lately.

"What about your team?" Josh put in.

Fire sparked in Kristen's big, wing-shaped eyes. "A litter of prairie rats stole them."

"So you left a prosperous business in Indiana to roost out *here*?" Bill asked.

"My pa had him a vision," she replied defiantly. "A vision of fruit orchards out west. And come hell or high water, I mean to make it come true."

Bill shook his head. She was billy-goat stubborn and brash as an Army mule.

"Out here, you'll get hell *and* high water, missy," he promised her. "I advise you to book passage back home."

Kristen's nostrils flared. "Advise your mother to teach you some manners, mister! Nobody asked for your advice. You ain't my husband."

"Give me a couple minutes," Bill boasted. "I just met you."

"You go to hell!" she repeated. "And dream on! Ten years of begging wouldn't get me to the altar with you."

"The marriage *bed* is far enough for me," Bill assured her. A second later Josh heard the decisive *whap* when she slapped Hickok hard—so hard his cigar flew three feet away.

Bill grinned, rubbing his sore cheek, as the young woman turned her back on him and stomped away.

"Miss?" called out a grinning brakeman. "We'll gladly give you a ride to Abilene. You can hire a team and come back for your wagon. It should be safe out here for a bit."

"Thank you," she replied stiffly. "We appreciate that. But please keep *this* awful, unmannerly brute with the fancy guns"—she pointed at Wild Bill—"far away from me."

"Yessum. He's a bad one, all right."

The brakeman winked at Bill, and both men grinned on the sly.

Now, thought Josh jealously, Bill's got him a plaything in Abilene. Or *thinks* he has—this one doesn't seem too damned charmed by him. But she gave *me* a nice smile.

Bill was still watching Miss Kristen McCoy of Fort Wayne, Indiana, as she rounded up her siblings. Hickok's sly grin irritated Josh.

"Hey, Bill?"

"Hey what?"

"C. J.," Josh said softly.

Hickok's grin was gone in a heartbeat. He went white as new gypsum, and Josh saw the panic light in his eyes. The legend of the West suddenly looked helpless and scared.

"Christ," Bill said hoarsely. "Where is she?"

"Just keeping you on your toes," Josh replied, heading back toward the train. Now he was wearing a sly grin of his own.

Chapter Four

Martha "Calamity Jane" Burke watched, jealous bile rising in her throat, while the one and only love of her young life made a damned fool of himself.

It was soft brained enough, Jane told herself, that Wild Bill would want to spend time in *any* town. She hated all of them, full of blue-nosed biddies and spineless, soft-bellied clerks. But why in Sam Hill would Wild Bill Hickok—one of the few men out here with a real set on him—mingle with all these mealymouthed peckerwoods? And in *this* raggedy-assed hole full of thieves and back shooters?

"Well anyhow," she informed the team of bays filling the traces of her buckboard. "That damned little blond hussy best not come between *this* dog and her meat!"

The weathered sideboards of Jane's rig advertised DOYLE'S HOP BITTERS: THE INVALID'S FRIEND AND HOPE! The conveyance sat just inside the narrow, shadowed mouth of a north-south cross alley. It debouched onto Texas Street, the main thoroughfare in drab but bustling Abilene.

By craning her leathery and sunburned neck, Jane had a good view of the red-brick train station just east of town. The diamond stack of a newly arrived locomotive still belched smoke and sparks; hissing steam billowed from the escape valves even as the passengers detrained.

"Bill, you're fighting your destiny, honey," Jane said.

Our destiny, she corrected herself. Our shared destiny.

Jane turned her right hand palm up and smiled as she stared at the long, curving line that bisected the pudgy palm. She recalled, with stomach-tingling pleasure, the words of that ancient *bruja* down in Old El Paso: *The dangerous man you love is meant to be yours alone. But the road to his heart will be long, lonely, and littered with bones.*

"And blondes," Jane spat out, staring at the mud-smeared woman and the grimy urchins clinging to her. Nose stuck in the air like she was *something*. But the little prissy bitch looked like

41

she had been rolling in a pigpen. Bill usually dallied with rich women and famous actresses and such. This one wasn't good enough to lace his boots.

Bill had not actually come near the woman since they both detrained. But Jane saw him eye-groping her, saw him giving young Joshua several gleaming yaller boys—looked like maybe forty dollars or so, la!—and Josh taking them to the woman.

Then Jane watched the two men lead their horses from a boxcar and aim for the livery stable.

"Hep!" Jane shouted to her team, slapping their glossy rumps with the reins. "Hep, hep!"

She drove in the opposite direction. Jane was banned from spending the night in most western towns. She had a slight tendency, once snockered, to liven things up with curses and bullets. But she had already located an excellent campsite near a spring-fed rill about three miles from town.

No one had told her Hickok would be returning to Abilene. But the fiddle-footed frontiersman had a way of showing up wherever the worst trouble reared its head. Sometimes he *became* the worst trouble.

And, of course, wherever Bill was in bad trouble, Jane made it a point to be near him. She had sent more than one yellow-bellied dry gulcher to his grave for trying to put the quietus on Bill.

Plenty more would be trying. Hell's a-poppin' hereabouts, Jane realized. She had seen reward notices everywhere, plastered up by the Kansas-Pacific Railroad. They solicited "any information whatsoever concerning the recent killings of KP employees in the Abilene area."

Calamity Jane's buckboard shuddered hard in the ruts. Abilene had changed little since the last time she was here. This boomtown had never bothered with fancy false fronts. Most of the buildings were just rough cottonwood logs chinked with mud. There stood the Alamo Saloon, where Bill had "held office" while sheriff.

And there, two doors away, stood the Drover's Cottage.

Seeing it, Jane shouted, "Haw!" to her team. For an idea had just occurred to her. One that tugged her fleshy lips into a smile.

Why in tarnal hell, she reasoned, should Bill get off scot-free just because she loved him? That randy son of a bitch needed cold water tossed on him!

The Drover's Cottage was a former saloon that had evolved into a rude hotel by adding a few small rooms, a board canopy, and duckboards out front to lure ladies across all the mud. Wild Bill would probably take a room there. Why not, Jane thought as a sly grin divided her homely face, have a little welcome ready for His Nibs, the lady slayer?

"Hey, bub! Over here!"

Jane whistled to a little boy passing by on the boardwalk, kicking an Arbuckle's coffee can. "Kid! Wanna make two bits real quick?"

The kid let his can roll into the street. But he hung fire when he saw how coyote ugly the woman was. And there was a huge .44 tucked into her sash.

"*Four* bits, you little rat!" Jane gave in.

"You bet, lady!"

"C'mere, then. I want you to take something to the Drover's Cottage for me."

The livery barn in Abilene was just as Bill recalled it except for a new stone water trough. The old hostler was straight out of Genesis. Bill and Josh found him in the tack room, pounding caulks into horseshoes.

"You ain't dead yet, Jeddiah?" Bill greeted the old-timer.

Old Jed squinted in the grainy light, his rheumy eyes slow to recognize the new arrivals.

"Well cuss my coup! Bill Goldang Hickok! *You* ain't dead yet neither, gunman?"

"I'm working on it, dad. Got room for two more critters?"

"Only if you'll touch me for luck, Bill."

Bill gave the codger a hearty grip. Then Hickok and Josh slipped their horses' bits and loosed the cinches, tossing the saddles onto racks in the tack room. They hung their bridles nearby on cans nailed to the wall.

Meantime, Old Jed gnawed a corner off his plug, got it juicing good, then cheeked his cud. He was too old to offer help when younger bucks were willing to work.

"This town got a sheriff now?" Bill asked.

"Ah-huh. One with a tinhorn badge and a cheese spine to match. As usual, he's off to 'court' in Newton. Got him a whore over that way, or so you'll hear folks say."

"He crooked or yellow?"

"Both, you ask me. But nobody ever does."

Josh watched the old man snap his quirt at a fly and squash it dead.

"Kiss for ya!" Jed gloated. "Bill ain't the only one can aim."

The two men led their horses into stalls and forked in some clean hay. Bill grabbed the grain scoop and helped himself, filling a nose bag for Fire-away.

"We'll want them both curried and rubbed down every day," Bill told the old man. "If the weather holds good, turn them out nights into the paddock."

Bill flipped the hostler a quarter eagle. "That suit you, old roadster?"

Jed bit the coin and then grinned, flashing yellow nubbins of teeth. "Right down to the ground!"

As the two men were leaving, Jed called out behind them, "Keep an eye on your back trail, Billy! This rat's nest has got lots worser since the days of fellas like you and Tom Smith."

Big, red-headed, hard-fisted Tom Smith was the first man to clean up Abilene and enforce a new no-gun law. But two homesteaders finally murdered him, and Wild Bill was hired in his place. "Sure glad to see you," Wild Bill would greet the cowboys. "But hand over those guns." Nor did Bill debate the order—any man who balked promptly got shot.

"For nine months I was the star man around here," Bill boasted to Josh. "Hundreds of thousands in cold cash changed hands. But there wasn't one holdup on my watch. And I did the only shooting."

"I know," Josh said. "But they've obviously scrapped that gun law." Josh glanced all around. "Everybody's armed to the teeth. Even half the women."

But clearly Bill was aware of that. He'd kept his black, broad-brimmed hat pulled low to cover his face. And the long gray duster Bill wore to protect his suit also hid his distinctive Colts.

Josh saw Bill watching everything and everyone from the corners of his eyes like a payroll guard. At one point Bill stopped to look over a deserted shack near the livery.

"Let's go visit the Western Union," Bill said, hitching his shell belt. "That shack inspires me, Longfellow. We'll lay a little diversion trap for the enemy."

Their boot heels knocked on the boardwalk, reminding Josh of a funeral march. Cowboys were in evidence everywhere, lounging in small groups and insulting one another with rough fondness. Josh noticed that woolly angora chaps, so common up in Montana, were replaced by the flat rawhide of warmer ranges. So far, no one seemed to recognize Hickok.

Josh and Bill turned quietly through a raw plank door into a cramped cubbyhole office. A timid little bald-headed man, wearing green eye-shades and a pair of sleeve garters, sat behind a deal counter recording an incoming message as a sounder tapped it out.

He hadn't heard anyone enter. He finished writing. Then he glanced up and spotted Hickok watching him from level, gunmetal eyes.

"Jesus, mister!"

The clerk started violently, his hands fluttering like nervous birds. "You scared the snot outta me!"

"Sorry," Bill told him insincerely. "Just want to send a telegram to Denver."

"Yessir. Denver it is."

Josh watched Bill fill out the message-trans-mission form.

"No code?" Josh said low.

Bill shook his head. "Not this time."

ALLAN: I'M AVOIDING THE HOTEL IN ABILENE. TOO DANGEROUS.
I'M STAYING IN A DESERTED SHACK BY THE FEED STABLE.

W. B. H.

47

But the *W. B. H.* signature, Josh knew, *was* a code in itself. It told Pinkerton to disregard the message. All legitimate messages Bill signed with a solitary *H*.

"We can't four-flush 'em forever," Bill told Josh after they'd left the telegraph office. "But maybe we can bluff long enough to make 'em show their hand. Take a room at the Drover's Cottage," he added. "Better use a summer name. All the rooms are ground floor. But tell the clerk you require a window for fresh air. That'll be my door. Anybody asks for your story, launder it."

Josh nodded and carried out the orders. Luck was with him, and the clerk put him in the back room, its single sash window opening onto an empty lot. It was easy for Bill to step lithely over the sash without being spotted.

"I'll flip you for the bed, kid," Bill said, glancing dubiously at the dingy room with its fly-specked window. There was a threadbare, rose-patterned carpet, a washstand with an enameled pitcher and bowl, a beat-up highboy, and two ladderback chairs, badly scarred from spurs.

"Floor might be safer," Bill added, noticing that the legs of the iron bedstead had been set in bowls of coal oil to keep off the bedbugs.

"You seen him yet?" Josh asked.

"Seen who?"

"The sniper."

"Never mind," Bill said. "The real question with him is, has he seen *me?*"

Three quick raps at the door killed the conversation.

"Hotel clerk, Mr. Croft. You have a message."

Croft was the name Josh signed on the register. Bill tapped Josh's shoulder and mouthed the words *get your gun ready*. Then Hickok faded back into the shadowed corner to the left of the door.

Josh slid out his pistol, thumbed back the hammer, made sure there was a cartridge in the chamber. Then he eased open the door a crack until he saw the bushy muttonchops of the desk clerk.

"Sir? Some little kid just brought this in. Said to give it to the young fellow with . . . ahh, with the cute little dimples, sir, were his words."

Josh flushed and accepted a folded note and a bottle of Old Taylor bourbon from the grinning clerk.

Josh banged the door shut. Bill stared at the bottle in the kid's hand. He snatched the note from Josh and read it aloud.

" 'Some of the toughest men run from what they need most. That skinny little blonde is just a snack, Wild Bill.' "

Bill looked at Josh. "It's signed 'A Full Meal.' "

"Man alive, Bill! She's found us!"

Hickok stood still as a pillar of salt, watching Josh and smoothing his mustache with one finger. Suddenly Bill laughed.

"Good one, kid! Jee-zus, you had me going there for a minute. Gimme that bottle, wouldja? 'Preciate it."

"Bill, it's *her*. I didn't do this, I swear!"

"Look, wiseass, the joke's gone far enough."

But Josh had crossed to the open window. A little boy in patched jeans was visible, cutting catty-corner across the empty lot toward Silver Street. Josh whistled the kid back.

"Hey, bub? Did *I* tell you to bring this bottle and note to the hotel?"

The kid's freckled face hovered just above the sash. "Nuh-un. A woman did."

Bill paled and stepped out of the shadows. "Ugly woman?" he pressed.

The kid nodded vigorously. "Stinky one, too, mister. Phew!"

Josh shooed the kid away. Bill smacked his forehead and groaned like a soul in torment. Then he handed one of his Colts to Josh.

"Oh, Christ, Longfellow! Will that woman hound me even to hell? Damnit all, just shoot me now! *Please*, kid, take pity and shoot me!"

Chapter Five

"Was he sure it's Hickok?" 'Bama Jones demanded.

"Sure, he's sure, porky," Ansel Logan shot back. "Perry even told me where he's staying."

"Perry don't know gee from haw."

"So what? He's also spineless. But he knows Hickok's face, all right. My grandmother knows it, Christ sakes."

"So it's Hickok," 'Bama conceded. "That don't mean Perry ain't been foxed. Hickok ain't as stupid as you look."

"Up yours," Logan said, walking back to his hobbled horse. He took the brass field glasses out of his near-side saddlebag.

A burning yellow sun was stuck high in the sky as if pegged there. Logan studied the rolling plains that stretched out in every direction, broken here and there only by a stunted cottonwood. The two men had taken up a good position in a natural sink well west of Abilene.

"See anything?" 'Bama demanded. The muzzle of his Big Fifty lay balanced on its bipod, ready to speak its deadly piece.

"I'm sick a waiting. Hell, it's been three hours."

"Just hold your water. I'm telling you, somebody from the KP will show."

Logan's eyes prowled the terrain. Despite his advice to 'Bama, Logan, too, was damn sick and tired of this placid, punkin-butter monotony. Sure, the pay was good. But what good was money if a man couldn't piss it away on a high, old time?

'Bama lay sprawled behind his rifle. With considerable effort and grunting, he rolled his huge bulk onto one elbow, larval face turned to watch Logan. He shaded his eyes from the sun.

"Hell, if you know where Hickok is holed up," 'Bama said in his lazy, take-your-time drawl, "do you mean to brace him?"

"Would *you* brace Hickok?"

"Me? Sure. When the Yellow River runs clear. But I ain't handy with a short iron like you are."

"Handy? Son, I'm miles past handy," Logan bragged, still watching the wide-open Kansas prairie through the glasses. "I'm death to the damn Devil, I am! But you see, the man who braces Hickok is a man secretly looking to die. And being ready to die is the weak half of being a man. The *strong* half is being able to kill so's you don't have to die. That's the part I do best at."

"So you say. So far, bo, I been doing all the blood work. But hey, gettin' back to Hickok. You just mean to leave him be? I mean, goddamn, Logan! Hickok ain't come to Abilene to buy beef. The man is here to kill *us*. You going to earn your pay or what?"

"S'matter, gettin' snow in your boots? Settle down. We know where Golden Curls is staying, I told you. Hickok don't know we got a man in Western Union. Why the hell would he?"

"Knowing stuff like this is why he ain't dead, that's why."

"Every lucky streak has to end," Logan insisted. "I already talked to some fellas in town. Gents that won't be riding winter range, so they'll be a little light in their pockets, you take my drift? They'd be happy as hogs in mud to go shares on that ten thousand dollar reward. So they'll be paying Hickok a nighttime visit."

'Bama said something else, but Logan missed it.

"How's 'at?" he said absently, for he was unable to believe what he had just spotted. Logan quickly adjusted the focus knob on his glasses.

"Hell and furies," he said a moment later. "It *is* a woman!"

53

Judd Cole

And what a woman. A little skinny, but pretty as four aces, and she shaped up right peart, Logan decided. The blond was driving a big Studebaker wagon east toward Abilene. Three towheaded kids rode in the bed.

"A woman?" 'Bama repeated. "You sure?"

"Sure as shooting. Have a look."

"She's a woman, all right," 'Bama agreed a moment later. "And damn easy on the eye."

"This is mighty providential, 'Bama! I been needing me a women—a night woman, I mean."

"Let it alone," 'Bama protested. "There's three pups with that bitch! Ain't no real man 'needs' no woman nor nothing else."

"Hell! *You* don't know sic 'em about what men require. It's been proved by them professors at them colleges in France and England, porky. Proved by them as knows! See, a man is just like a volcano. He's got to have him a woman now and again, got to release the pressure inside him, or else he'll explode."

"Then get you a whore in town. Thissen's got kids with her."

Ansel gave a hard, tight-lipped smile straight as a seam. He started to tighten the girth on his saddle.

"So? Let 'em watch and learn. I ain't gonna hurt them *or* the little gal. Just a quick poke, is all. That's a man's na'chral right, innit?"

* * *

Capt. Jules Bledsoe, Fifth Cavalry Regiment, sat his saddle looking as solid as a meeting house. Five enlisted men were fanned out around him, their horses rigged light for fast travel.

"There's two of them," he finally announced, lowering his field glasses. "I only spotted them because they sky-lined themselves. Something's caught their attention to the north, that's why they're being so careless about watching their rear. The moment one of them turns around, he'll spot us."

"Is it the snipers, sir?" asked a Negro corporal. Like the rest, he carried little more equipment than a rifle, ammo belts, and a bedroll strapped to his saddle.

"Has to be, Jimmy. The fat one's got a Big Fifty with a scope and bipod."

"Then they sure's hell ain't buff hunters," said a leather-faced sergeant wearing an eye patch. "Let's put at 'em, sir."

"Knock the sand off your cartridges," Bledsoe ordered, for the Spencer carbine was a good killing rifle, but its copper shells were prone to jam easily. "Hold wide intervals during movement to contact. If they spot us, take up an avoidance pattern. We already know that sniper could shoot the eyes out of a buzzard at a thousand yards."

The men carried out these orders with an efficient, business-as-usual manner. Jules Bledsoe was a former Texas Ranger who had whipped even the fiercest Comanches into submission. All five of his men had been handpicked by Bledsoe, the fighting elite of the U.S. Army's new quick-strike regiments. They had ridden out from Fort Riley with only one urgent order: Kill the sniper or snipers terrorizing the Kansas-Pacific Railroad.

"Move out!" Bledsoe ordered. "And get ready for a chase. Once they spot us, they'll for sure rabbit. They won't go toe-to-toe with six of us."

"Logan!" 'Bama protested as the former circus shootist stepped up and over, reining his horse toward the north. "Let that woman go, damnit! It ain't smart to show yourself."

Logan waved him off. But before he could spur his horse, both men heard the sudden, hollow thudding of approaching hooves.

Logan slewed around in his saddle, then felt a cold fist squeeze his heart.

"Chee-*rist*!"

Six weathered, grim-faced soldiers were bearing down on him in a classic pincer's trap!

'Bama's Sharps was set up in the opposite direction. He had a dead aim, but Logan knew he was slow and clumsy—he'd never get that gun turned around in time to stop these blue-bloused avengers.

Even as the first carbine cracked, shooting a neat hole through his saddle fender, Logan went into action.

He leaped down, slapped his horse on the rump, then hit the ground rolling fast. Each time he rolled onto his back, he gave a little push, up and out of the deep grass, and tossed off a snap shot. And each time he fired, a soldier flew from his horse, face frozen in surprise.

Nor was any of the six shots a body hit. Each slug punched into the center of the forehead just below the soldier's hat. From long experience with a short iron, Logan knew that only a shot to the brain guaranteed a one-bullet kill. The heart was hidden and tucked away, but the brain was always vulnerable to a crack shot.

"I'll be goin' to hell!" 'Bama shouted. "You plugged the whole caboodle!"

"Who's doing the blood work *now*?" Ansel boasted, thumbing reloads into his cylinders.

"You blew away *six* soldiers!" 'Bama yelped. "Pow! Pow! Pow! *Jee*-zus!"

"Soldiers? Bosh! Buncha boys with their pants tucked into their boots," Logan boasted.

"Buncha dead boys now, bo," 'Bama chortled.

Logan cast a wistful glance at the blonde in the bouncing wagon, ideas popping in his mind like firecrackers.

"She can't see our faces from here. I best not go closer to her right after this turkey shoot," he decided reluctantly.

"Ah, she'll keep until another time. *Damn*, Logan! How can a man shoot six targets that fast?"

57

"I draw just as fast as I shoot," Logan assured him. "You still frettin' about Wild Bill Hickok?" Logan's tone mocked those last three words.

"Partner," 'Bama assured him, "after what I just seen? Hey, I ain't worried about nothing."

Chapter Six

The special courier sent from Denver by Allan Pinkerton arrived one day after Bill and Josh began their dangerous sojourn in Abilene.

Pinkerton's letter confirmed what both friends already suspected. Bill was indeed caught in the middle of a bloody railroad war—though, of course, no railroad in America would publicly admit that fact.

The Kansas-Pacific, Pinkerton reported, was expanding its northern route through Kansas to include more cowtowns like Hays City; meantime, the equally powerful Santa Fe Railroad would soon begin a new southern route through Kansas. Their goal, Pinkerton noted, was to drive the cattle trade (namely the vast feedlots) south from Abilene to Dodge City.

"Whoever takes this hand," Bill had commented with a grim face when he finished the letter, "will bust the bank. And the loser will be up Salt River without any profit for their investment."

Bill added that this was far from your usual scrap over a few parcels of land. This was a war to the death to see who took title to the West.

"And *we* get to witness it firsthand," Josh marveled. "Man alive, Bill! This is history happening! This'll be the biggest story I ever filed. Bigger than Vogel's ice machine, bigger than the Kinkaid County War even!"

"Get that glory light outta your eyes, kid," Bill warned him. "Just cause you got the drop on a scum bucket in Miles City doesn't mean you got divine protection. Could be, the only thing that gets filed will be our obituaries."

Bill's point was driven home forcefully by a newspaper account, one day later, of the bloody massacre of six soldiers west of Abilene. And Kristen McCoy was named as a witness, albeit a distant one.

" 'All six men,' " Josh read aloud from the *Abilene Chronicle*, " 'were killed by one man with a handgun, yet at rifle range. And each bullet was so precisely aimed, according to Doctor Levy, that all six struck their targets in virtually the same spot, the exact center of the forehead. According to Miss McCoy, who admits she was not close enough to describe the lone marksman, all six shots were fired in about four or five seconds.' "

Josh looked at Bill. "Holy Hannah!"

He folded up the newspaper and crammed it back into his saddlebag. It was late morning, and the two friends had ridden out "to get the lay of the land," as Bill put it. They rode out early, for by now Bill assumed word was out that Hickok was back in Abilene, looking for the grave he somehow missed last time.

"Damn, Longfellow," Bill mused when Josh finished reading. "This trail's taking enough turns to make a cow cross-eyed."

"Whad'ya mean?"

Bill's eyes stayed in constant scanning motion as he replied. Looking for movement, reflections, smoke, spooked animals.

"These killings are different than the others, that's what I mean. We already knew we're up against a mystery sniper with a sure-hit rifle. One who can shoot straight for a country mile. But what kind of marksman could drop a half-dozen top-notch soldiers as if they were green recruits. And do it *with a pistol?*"

"That would take a Bill Hickok," Josh suggested quietly.

"Or a man good enough to kill him. Christ," Bill said, "I *knew* Jules Bledsoe. I fought Comanches alongside him once when I was a driver for the Overland Stage Company. He taught me how to wing-shoot while changing locations. Jules was one of the best men on the frontier."

Josh felt it just as surely as Bill did: the gut-tickling sense that, even now, they were in the crosshairs of an assassin's weapon.

"Bill?" Josh decided now was the time for some answers. "Do you still think you know who the rifle sniper is, at least?"

Bill nodded. "That's an affirmative. I know of only one man who can kill at the distances that've been reported. He goes by the moniker of 'Bama Jones. He was once the most celebrated and feared sniper in the Confederate States Army. Us Billy Yanks called him Boneyard Jones and Old Drop-a-lot."

"He's good, huh?" Josh pressed eagerly, already composing his next story.

"Good? Hell, no, you ink-slinging idiot! He's as low-down dirty and mean as they come. Mister, I mean one kill-crazy son of a bitch! He's credited with more than a thousand kills during the war."

Josh goggled. "Straight goods, Bill?"

"My hand to God, kid! He could shadow an army on the march, stay so far back that nobody ever saw him. 'Bama could thin out an army better than dysentery. And guess what else?"

"What?"

"That deadeye killing machine could be laying a bead on *your* lights as we speak. Not to mention his pistol-packing pard, whoever the hell he is."

A solitary bead of sweat trickled out from Josh's hairline. Bill reined in, and Josh followed suit. For a long time Bill just sat there, his fathomless blue eyes again reading the level horizon.

"Tell you anything?" Josh asked.

"Looking for a man or two out here," Bill said, "is like trying to find a sliver in an elephant's ass."

"What about your plan with the deserted shack in town?" Josh asked. "Still think somebody will attack it to get you?"

Bill nodded. "That telegraph clerk is bent. I'd guess somebody will strike as soon as tonight. I'll be waiting."

Bill skinned the paper back from a cheroot, scowling now.

"On top of two expert killers, we got Calamity Jane out here somewhere. We're caught between a rock and a hard place, kid. At least a bullet is *quick*."

"What do we do now?"

Bill scratched a phosphor to life with his thumbnail and lit the cigar. He pressured Fire-away into motion with his knees.

"We palaver with the McCoy girl, that's what. She witnessed the rubout of the soldiers. The newspaper says she's squatting on an abandoned quarter-section north of Abilene. We can find her easy."

Bill kicked Fire-away from a trot to a canter.

"Yeah, well Kristen McCoy ain't so fond of you," Josh called out behind him, hurrying to catch up.

"Jesus, kid, that leaves me a broken man. Listen, you young fool, I'm looking for information, not a wife. Now quit flapping your lips and keep a weather eye out."

Bill was right. In less than an hour of easy riding, he and Josh rode into sight of the abandoned soddy where the orphaned McCoy clan had taken up residence.

"Gotta be it," Bill said. "There's her wagon, and no team. She must have hired one to haul it here."

"Won't they throw her out?" Josh asked.

"Not if this section is a relinquishment," Bill said, "which it appears to be. She can pay any back taxes and file a new claim."

Bill grinned and pointed ahead. "Look! She's already improving the place. Gone into business."

Josh saw a crude sign made from scrap wood nailed to a cottonwood. Scrawled charcoal letters proclaimed FRUIT TREE SEEDLINGS FOR SALE!

The two men rode up slowly. The trio of towheads were playing with a jar of butterflies in front of the low, one-story dwelling. They stared with hostile eyes at the new arrivals.

"Morning, kids!" Bill called out cheerfully. "Your sister to home?"

"None a your damn beeswax, mister!"

The speaker was the same belligerent seven-year-old boy who called them yahoos a few days earlier.

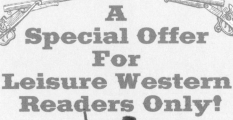

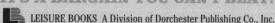

Get Four Books Totally
F R E E* —
A Value between
$16 and $20

Tear here and mail your FREE* book card today!

PLEASE RUSH
MY FOUR FREE*
BOOKS TO ME
RIGHT AWAY!

LeisureWestern Book Club
P.O. Box 6613
Edison, NJ 08818-6613

AFFIX
STAMP
HERE

"Mind if I look inside?"

"Hell yes, it ain't your house!"

Bill let Fire-away prance backward a few steps. Hickok stared at the little trooper, who scowled right back, lower lip puffed out defiantly.

"You win, shorty," Bill finally surrendered, trying to keep a straight face. "I know the better man when I meet him. C'mon, Josh. This mite's just too tough for us."

They started to wheel their horses around as if to leave. But the kid—tickled pink at this praise—suddenly relented.

"Hey, mister? Kristen went down to the creek. It's back of the house."

Bill touched the brim of his hat. " 'Preciate it, shorty. You're all man."

"Damn straight, Jack!"

"That little son of trouble requires a cowhide across his sitter," Bill grumbled as the two men trotted their horses around the soddy. "Nervy little half-pint. Brash, just like his big sis."

Neither man spotted the weed-sheltered creek until they had practically ridden right into it. Josh caught a glimpse of a faded blue anchor-print dress—clean now—hanging from a chokecherry bush.

Lord God, Josh thought. But even as he realized their mistake, he spotted the naked woman in the middle of the creek.

Josh's jaw dropped open in pure awe and astonishment. Even Wild Bill, whose eyes were far more accustomed to such sights, sat there greedily taking in this erotic vignette.

Kristen had raised both arms overhead to twist water from her wet blond ropes of hair. *How*, Josh marveled, could a gal so slim and fine-boned have such full and heavy breasts?

Beside him, Wild Bill swallowed audibly.

"Kid," Bill said quietly, "nothing focuses the mind like a naked woman, huh?"

Josh studied her wet, mother-of-pearl skin and wordlessly agreed. He'd read an Eastern tale once where a Hindu wise man summed up all of human history: "They were born; they were wretched; they died." But obviously that fellow, Josh told himself, never spotted Kristen McCoy bare-butt naked.

Unfortunately, she noticed her secret admirers before they could nudge their horses a few discreet steps back. She gave a little yelp and dropped beneath the protective screen of water.

"*You* again!" she hollered, shaking a fist at Wild Bill. "Always pushing in where you have no business, ain't you? And now turned into a sick, sneaking spy."

Her cornflower-blue eyes accused both men. Josh could almost whiff her anger.

"Now, darlin', calm down," Bill said soothingly. "We aren't spying; we just want to ask you some—"

"Mister, I know spying when I see it. I didn't just fall off the turnip wagon!"

"No," Bill agreed. "It was a Studebaker, as I recall."

"Damn you! Just who are you anyway?"

"The name is Hickok, missy. Jim Hickok of Troy Grove, Illinois."

A vagrant breeze chose that moment to tug Wild Bill's long gray duster aside. This exposed the pearl handle of a Peacemaker. Kristen stared at it.

"Hickok? As in . . . Wild Bill Hickok?"

Josh watched Bill nod. Here it comes, Josh thought, feeling a stab of jealousy. All women are alike when it comes to famous men. Now she'll be all over him like cheap perfume.

"You," Kristen told Bill in a cool, level tone, "are just a cold-blooded killer. My father, may he rest in peace, told me all about you and men like you. Vain, heartless murderers who think you're little tin gods above the law."

Bill just sat there like unwanted furniture. "Opinions vary," he told her calmly.

But Josh could detect a tone of rising anger in his voice. Wild Bill would let anyone call him a killer because it was true. Kristen, however, had just called him a murderer—a word only a woman would dare use to his face.

"It's a judgment," she retorted, "not an opinion. My father was the wisest man I ever knew. You know what else he said about you?"

"You mean, about my good looks?"

"Yes, no doubt you think so. Well, you are nice to look at, Mister Hickok, though I prefer a man's hair to be shorter than my own."

"Kid," Bill said, "was that a compliment?"

"I've heard better," Josh replied.

"What my father said about you," Kristen forged on, ignoring both of them, "is that you are America's epitaph, Hickok! So either get off my property, or go ahead and kill me. Because you'll *have* to kill me before you rape me, gunslinger!"

Bill's complete failure to elicit any information from Kristen McCoy left the Pinkerton op no other choice. His only slim hope now was that deserted shack on the outskirts of Abilene.

By now, Bill told Josh, everybody in town knew Hickok was back. So Josh rode back first, and Bill waited until after sundown. He turned Fire-away into the livery corral, then quickly rubbed him down and pitched in some hay. Bill returned to the hotel room through the window.

"I know how these assassination jobs work," Bill told Josh as the two men slipped through the shadowed backlots of town. "That's why nobody's managed to plant me yet, knock on wood. But the timing is always tricky, kid."

It was an unusually mild night for autumn, clearly moonlit, the air warm and soft as the breath of a young girl. The two men closed in on the shack, sticking to the shadow cast by the big livery barn across Texas Street.

Bill pointed at the weather-rawed shack, easy to make out in silvery moonlight. It had one window, minus glass, one door, and a tin chimney with a conical cap.

"It's a natural death trap, kid," Wild Bill said. "And I want *you* to go on inside."

Josh gawped in the moonlight. "Me?"

"Sure. Ain't you the terror of Miles City?"

Bill's white teeth gleamed like foxfire for a moment, and Josh knew he was grinning in the dark. Bill took off Josh's hat, put it on his own head, and plopped his own on the kid's head.

"That's the gait, Longfellow! You're the meat that lures the tiger. Look, here's the way of it. The bad fellas, whoever the hell they are, have been watching the shack. They're watching it now, I'll warrant, and they know it's empty. So they have to see 'me' go inside. You're almost exactly my size. Here, take my duster, too."

Josh felt belly flies stirring when he walked boldly out into the moonlit street, then slipped into the shack. Mice skittered into the corners as the crooked plank door scraped on the dirt floor.

Bill had already warned him how the attack would most likely go. Since there were no rear exits, the attackers would simply burn any occupants out, cutting them down with bullets as they escaped perforce through door or window. Bill had ordered Josh to stay put, no matter what, until he gave the hail.

Time ticked by slow, and Josh heard only the monotonous crackle of insects and the hissing murmur of wind. Heat lightning began to flash. At one point, maybe around 2 A.M. or so, thunder suddenly cracked, and a soft rain sizzled on the roof of the shack. It stopped after a few minutes.

Josh didn't doze, but he went into a daze like men who are saddle sleepy. Then, perhaps an hour after the rain stopped, all hell broke loose.

Josh's eyelids had grown heavy from boredom. A burning lantern flew through the open window frame and crashed against the back wall so abruptly that he gasped like a scared maiden. In three heartbeats, the old tinderbox shack *whooshed* into flames.

Josh's first instinct was to bolt to safety. But he fought down that lethal mistake, remembering Bill's order.

The paralyzing fear passed. The reporter had his pinfire revolver in hand as he edged up to the window and peeked outside.

The scene, through gathering smoke, was bedlam. Josh saw three or four figures on horseback, rifles glinting in the moonlight, waiting in the street for Hickok to emerge from the burning shack. In the crackling flames, their horses crow-hopped in panic, showing the whites of their eyes.

And there! There was the man Josh came west to write about. Wild Bill, moving up on the riders cat-footed from the inky fathoms of shadow behind them. Highbrows scoffed at dime novels, Josh knew, yet only look—*there* was the cover painting for one right there, and it was real as death and taxes.

"Toss down your guns or die now!" Wild Bill commanded with unmistakable authority. Josh knew he hoped to interrogate a live prisoner.

But fate dealt Bill the wrong hand. Two of the riders immediately reined around and escaped in opposite directions while, simultaneously, two more unleashed a hail of lead at Wild Bill. Before Josh could even knock the thong off the hammer of his pinfire, Bill blew both gunsels out of their saddles.

"Aww, damn!" Josh heard Bill curse, even as the reporter bolted, coughing hard, from the burning shack.

Wild Bill made sure the riders weren't doubling back. Then he squatted on his ankles and studied the dead men in the spectral moonlight. Josh could smell the powerful stink of their heavy Mexican tobacco, stronger even than cigar stink.

"Prob'ly don't matter anyhow, kid," Bill said, sounding like he'd been punched hard but not quite dropped. "I don't know either one of them. But look how greasy their clothes are. Smell that Mex tobacco? Hell, even Indians scorn that crap. And look how their boots are tied with burlap. I'd wager these boys are no connection to our sniper and our pistol expert. Just local chawbacons out for the reward on my hide."

"The hell's going on?" somebody shouted, and more voices bubbled in the distance. Josh saw swinging lanterns approaching like fireflies.

Bill stood up and thumbed two reloads into his cylinder. He swore again, but without anger. Josh noticed that Hickok was one to rile cool, never losing his temper.

"What do we do now, Longfellow? Sit and play the harp? Well, let's fade. These two ain't our mess; let somebody else clean it up."

Chapter Seven

It wasn't Wild Bill Hickok's way to push when a thing wouldn't move. So when he failed to draw out the two killers in Abilene, he decided on a bold new strategy.

"Kid," he told Josh on the day after the shoot-out at the shack, "obviously we can't stay our killer's hand. So we're going to follow his bullet back to the gun."

Josh, busy at the desk blotting a sheet of writing with sand, translated Bill's sentence in his mind. Then he paled slightly and said, "What you mean is—we have to get deliberately shot at, right?"

"A man has to go outside to check the weather, am I right? So we have to take jobs with the Kansas-Pacific—we do that, and we've got the keys to the mint."

"Or the morgue," Josh muttered.

Bill cast a regretful glance into the mirror, admiring his blond curls and carefully trimmed mustache.

"They'll have to go," he carped. "We can't know who's crooked and who's straight. So we'll take summer names and hire on as two common, bagline bums out of work."

Bill wrote out a short message for Pinkerton, then converted it into alphanumeric code. "Send this to Allan," he told Josh. "We'll have him hire us on with the KP so we get added to the local work-crew roster."

Thus, only one day later, two new laborers rode the work train out of Abilene, bound for the spur line being built by the Kansas-Pacific. Wild Bill had hired on as Liam O'Brien, a common navvy on the grading crew. Josh, who had obviously never handled a shovel or spike maul in his young life, was made water boy at Chinaman's wages— half the hourly wage of white workers.

As luck would have it, the hard-cussing English foreman took an instant dislike to both new arrivals. He was a big, barrel-chested, florid-faced Cockney named Wilson, a barracks-room bully with slack jowls and trouble-seeking eyes.

Wild Bill had been assigned to follow the mule teams pulling the iron-bladed graders. His job was to shovel gravel and dirt fill into uneven spots along the newly graded track bed. Such workers were required to move fast, avoid conversations, and take no smoke breaks until authorized by Wilson.

Now and then, Wilson pushed up close to Wild Bill and berated him soundly.

"O'Brien, you worthless Irish sot! You aren't digging potatoes back in Cork County, paddy! Wield that shovel like you *own* a pair, you bloody mick!"

Nor did Josh fare any better. His slender shoulders bent precariously under the sagging weight of a wooden yoke, a pail of water dangling from each end. In town, the cowboys had scorned Josh's ready-to-wear boots; out here, the workingmen scorned his pale skin and uncallused hands, his educated speech. Wilson promptly dubbed him "Little Miss Pink Cheeks."

Near the end of their first work day, Josh was blistered and bone weary. He could tell that Bill was no better off. Hickok faced more danger in one month than most men faced all their lives. But he was not conditioned to hard, supervised labor.

"Hey, Pinky!" a burly laborer bellowed at Josh. "I'm spitting cotton! Hustle up with that damn water, you laggard."

"Worthless little weak sister," Wild Bill added, and Josh scowled at him.

When he found a moment, Josh stopped beside Bill.

"No sniper attacks today," Josh said. "Man alive! I'd almost rather get shot than haul this water rig another day."

Bill was smooth shaven, his hair so closely cropped it was dark. He wore baggy coveralls and a pillow-tick work cap. He removed the cap and whipped the dust from it. His eyes, closed to slits against the sun, studied the endless plains.

"Buck up, Longfellow. Our shooters will tip their hand sooner or later. I'll lay you two to one they hit us today or tomorrow. There's a surveying crew right out in front of us, tempting them."

Bill's eyes were tracking something just north of the work site. Josh followed his gaze and recognized it immediately—a bone wagon. They dotted the buffalo ranges now that the new fertilizer plants paid five dollars a ton for buffalo bones. The men who collected them were mostly filthy scavengers who worked for whiskey money.

"Only two men in that crew," Bill muttered as if making pointless dinner talk. "There's usually three or four."

"O'Brien!" Wilson's bullhorn voice rasped. "Pinky! Who told you two girls to slack off? The day's still a pup, you blokes get back to work."

Bill ran a dry tongue over chapped lips. He picked up his shovel. "Well, kid, back to the salt mines."

But Josh watched him send his gaze out toward the bone wagon one more time before Bill bent to resume his labor.

* * *

"There's no dang hurry on the next surveyor," 'Bama Jones insisted. "Better safe than sorry. I've killed three in the last four weeks. What I'm wondering, where the hell is Hickok?"

"Why don't you *wonder* where past years go?" Ansel Logan shot back. "It'd be just as sensible. Never mind exactly where Hickok is, porky. You're some pumpkins with a Big Fifty, all right. But you're also hawg stupid."

"The hell's bitin' on you today?"

"Never mind me. One thing's for damn sure: Hickok left his calling card in Abilene a couple days ago. Drilled Jeb Johnson and Dill Stover right through their lights. Course, *I* kilt six at one go, all soldiers."

'Bama only grunted at this. He and Logan shared the board seat of a big farmer's wagon pulled by oxen. 'Bama wore a huge slouch hat and was fifty pounds heavier now than during the war, when he'd hardly ever eaten a square meal.

Each time the big conveyance lurched, old buffalo bones scraped and clattered behind them. So far this had proved an excellent dodge—bone scavengers, like any parasites on the frontier, went virtually ignored while wandering at will. As for locating bones: The herds always followed ancient migration trails, as regular as the equinox. Since hunters followed them, bones were literally easy pickings.

"Look at them wage hustlers," Ansel said with contempt.

He kept the reins in his right hand and used his left to point toward the railroad work crew on their left flank.

"Taking guff all day for a buck and a half," Logan said. A smile twisted his lips, and he added, "Plus all the danger from *us*. Honest labor don't pay, 'Bama. No sir!"

"I don't like the way that one navvy is staring at us," 'Bama complained. "Damn my hide if he don't look familiar."

"So *let* the two-bit wage slave stare. I got better things to think on than a damn shit-heel working-man. Like that little gal we seen the day I planted them soljers."

"Set it to music, bo!" 'Bama complained. "She's all you been talking about. Christ, are you apron tied?"

"Ain't her *apron* I'm wantin' to take off her, you ignut cracker. Damn but she was silky satin, all right. I got my eyes peeled for *that* little piece."

"Well you best keep 'em peeled for Hickok," 'Bama suggested. "I'll take care of the surveyors. You just keep Hickok off us, that's all I ask. He's close, Logan, damn close by us, and that's pure dee fact. What he done in Abilene the other night was just chicken fixens."

For the next two days it rained in biblical torrents on the Great Plains.

Bleeding Kansas

Gray, driving sheets of rain pounded the flats and swelled the rivers and creeks. Grading railbeds was out of the question, so the workers remained at the end-of-track tent city. Bill and Josh played long games of poker, using a nail keg for a table.

"Kid," Bill remarked as the rain began to slacken on the second day, "work won't start up for at least a day so the mud can dry out. I want you to ride into Ellsworth."

Ellsworth was the next cowtown west of Abilene, perhaps three hours ride from there. By now Josh had the cooped-up fever and welcomed the assignment.

"Why?" he asked.

"You're going to send another telegram to Pinkerton," Bill explained. "I just remembered something. Western Union just installed a big new storage drum in Denver. It holds all telegrams sent between this region's stations. Leaves a back-up copy punched out in perforations. Pinkerton has access to it."

"I get it," Josh said, pulling on his damp boots. "Pinkerton can check all the messages that originate from Abilene."

Bill nodded. He had opened a saddlebag to remove his Colts and clean them.

"That telegraph clerk might be in touch with a superior. Somebody representing the Santa Fe Railroad. We need to find a link, get some names."

So Josh dutifully cut his horse out from the camp corral and carried out his mission without mishap. It was still squalling when he left. But by the time he returned, just before nightfall, the sky had cleared.

"Good work," Bill told him, breaking out the poker deck. "Good weather means our sniper will soon be back. And I miss clean sheets. But, you know, Longfellow? I confess I feel safer out here than in Abilene."

Bill filled a tin cup with Old Taylor and fired up a cheroot. "Matter fact, kid, wasn't for that damn blowhard Wilson, I might keep this job awhile. Blisters kill a man lots slower than bullets.

"Five card draw," Bill added, "one-eyed jacks wild. Yessir, this life could be worse. We could—"

"Aww, *hell!*" Josh cut him off. He rose and stepped to the open fly of their two-man tent. "It's C. J., Bill! Jeez, she's found us! She musta spotted me coming back from Ellsworth."

Bill chuckled as he dealt out cards. "Kid, you got to learn when to give a joke a rest. It was funny the first time you pulled it."

But in the silence following his remark, both men heard it: a raucous, drunken female voice singing.

Buffalo Gal, won't you
come out tonight,
come out tonight,
come out tonight. . . .

80

"God kiss me!"

Josh watched Bill scramble to blow out the kerosene lantern.

A six-shooter sounded, and Calamity Jane roared out, "Bill Hickok, you purty hunk o' man-flesh, I'm a-comin' to climb all over you, boy!"

"Get jobs with the railroad," Josh said scornfully, quoting Bill. "We do that, and we got the keys to the mint."

"Oh, Christ," Bill moaned in the darkened tent. "She's drunker than the lords of creation. Keep her the hell away from me, kid!"

Chapter Eight

Jane's six-shooter barked again. Already, Josh could see half the workcamp turning out to see what all the ruckus was about.

"Let's pull a cork, boys!" Jane roared out in her voice that could fill a canyon. "Dang garn it, Wild Bill Hickok is here someplace. And by grab, I mean to sniff that critter out!"

"She's horny as a Texas steer," Bill said low, hiding behind the tent flap. "And drunk. I'd rather face down a she-grizz with cubs."

"Let's have us a fandango!" Calamity Jane bellowed, halting her buckboard right outside Josh and Bill's tent. "C'mon, you railroad chuckleheads! This gal's lookin' for some *men!*"

Josh watched his foreman, Wilson, come blustering up to Jane.

"*You're* a woman?" Wilson demanded. He stood hip cocked before the buckboard, his face hard as granite in the day's dying light. "Christ, you look like you been rode hard and put away wet, you ugly hell hag."

"Whew! Ain't *he* in a pet!" Jane exclaimed. "Shoo! Don't come a-puffin' and a-blowin' at *me*, you ignorant British shit heap!"

Josh looked at the big knife tucked into Jane's left peg boot.

"Pitch it to hell, you ugly witch," Wilson shot back, wagging a stubby finger at her. "This is property of the Kansas-Pacific Railroad. Now clear out before I take a blacksnake whip to your leather hide."

Josh heard Bill chuckle beside him. "Big mistake, boss," Hickok said.

Jane's wind-cracked lips parted in a howl of scorn. "Why, you double-poxed hound! I'll learn you some manners, you half-faced limey groat!"

Jane fired once, twice, and both ends of Wilson's walrus mustache disappeared. Her third shot snapped his belt and dropped his trousers around his ankles.

"Blimey!" Wilson stood there in his sagging long johns, too frightened to move.

Jane trembled with mirth. "All holler and no heart, eh, Jeebs? Turn around, you tea-sipping lout, and I'll blow your goldang trapdoor open!"

By now Wilson was trying to flee. But his trousers twisted around his ankles, and he sprawled in the mud. Wilson was hated by every man in camp, so his predicament evoked paroxysms of mirth.

"Say, boys!" Jane yelled. "I'll betcha Mister Union Jack here has got him a little-bitty tally-whacker. Let's take a peek at it."

Jane raised her .44, pretending she was about to shoot his long johns off.

"No," Wilson begged. "Christ sakes, no!"

By now everyone, Bill and Josh included, was convulsed with mirth. An eye blink later, with no warning, Wilson's head exploded in a spray of blood and bone shards!

It wasn't until some seconds later that the sound of the long-distance rifle shot reached camp.

"Suffering Moses!" cried Calamity Jane, suddenly shocked sober.

Now Josh understood—Bill had meant it literally when he said he was going to "follow the bullet back to the gun."

Gouts of blood were still spuming from Wilson's head as Bill, ignoring the threat of Jane, hurried outside.

Calamity Jane, still thunderstruck, didn't appear to recognize Bill in that grainy twilight—not in work clothes and with his hair and mustache clipped off.

"Don't move him yet!" Bill commanded.

Everyone was still too stunned to worry about why the new laborer was suddenly taking charge. Josh stepped outside, too.

"Where's Wild Bill?" Jane demanded, recognizing him.

"Out scouting," Josh lied.

"Wilson was standing with his right side facing south," Bill told Josh in a quiet voice. "The bullet went in just above the right ear. The exit wound is below the left eye. That means the bullet's trajectory wasn't straight—the shooter fired from a spot slightly southwest of here."

Jane could hear none of this. "Looks like he's beyond a poultice, boys," she told the two men.

Bill stood up and turned to face southwest. Impressed, Josh watched the savvy frontiersman "sight a line" to the ambush point, just as a surveyor might.

"I found it," Bill told Josh confidently. "There's just enough light in the sky to make it out—see?"

Josh stared, hardly able to make out anything beyond the middle distances. But he thought he saw it, too—a slight rise topped by a few scrub trees.

Calamity Jane squinted at the worker who called himself Liam O'Brien. Feeling her curious eyes on him, Bill gave Josh the high sign and they went back to their tent.

"It's 'Bama," Bill said urgently. "Kid, that knoll is at least 1500 yards out. *No*body could manage a shot at that distance, in this light, but him. Bet you a dollar to a doughnut hole he's got a scope, too."

While he said all this, Bill was buckling his shell belt and guns on.

"You're going out there *now?*" Josh asked. "With full dark coming on?"

"Full moon tonight," Bill replied, palming his cylinders to check the action. "Plus, this ground is soft from the rain lately. Sign will be easy to read."

"Oh, God, no!" Josh pleaded, peeking through the tent flap. "Jane's coming to our tent!"

"She's all yours, kid," Wild Bill said, pulling up the rear of the tent to escape. "Give her a big, sloppy kiss for me!"

"Bill, no, wait up! Take me with you!"

"Sorry, Longfellow," Bill said, already scuttling under the tent. "Every man to his duty! Buck up, trooper!"

"You got the easy part!"

"Hell, I know that," Bill called back. "All *they* can do is kill me."

Bill had no desire to traipse all over hell, in the dark, searching for two top-notch killers. Mainly, he wanted to confirm a nagging suspicion.

Although Fire-away wanted to run out the kinks, Bill kept him reined in to a slow trot. There were too many gopher holes hereabouts that could easily snap a running horse's leg.

It was a long uphill grade to that knoll: Bill could feel Fire-away's shoulder muscles straining. He stopped several times to cool the gelding before the crest—the night wind had turned cold, and too much sweat would chill any horse.

Bill crossed a creek on a shallow gravel ford, then rode through a patch of stubby *palo duro*. He tried to clear his mind of the clutter of thoughts, tried instead to focus intensely on the here and now.

Nonetheless, he couldn't help feeling his own vulnerability in this generous moonwash. Bill's skin pimpled with fear. Imagination's loom wove bloody images; over and over, Bill's inside eye saw Wilson's head exploding like a melon. Out west, a man had wheeling distance, all right. But that very vastness could also seal a bloody fate.

Bill had great faith in his horse. He was a swift dodger, an adept twister, and of good bottom to endure. Bill often bragged that Fire-away could turn on a two-bit piece and give back fifteen cents in change. But no horse could duck a bullet that was already in flight.

Fire-away kept wanting to cut grass. So Bill stopped briefly and fed the horse a few handfuls of corn from his saddle pockets. But eventually he reached the crest of the knoll, covered by scrubby dwarf willows.

It was easy to put together the clear sign. He could see precisely where the two men waited, also where the sniper had planted his bipod in the dirt. A pair of human tracks led back to waiting horses.

They had then ridden off to the northwest. Bill followed the trail for about an hour and finally found what he was looking for: the place where the two killers had tied their horses to the back of a wagon and continued on.

For a long moment Bill sat in the chilly wind, recalling those "bone scavengers" he had witnessed earlier. The wind rose to a shrieking howl, blasting Bill's face with hard-driven grit.

"The bastards rode right past us earlier," Bill told Fire-away. "Bold as a big man's ass."

Bill resisted the urge to keep going. This was no country for sneaking up on a man. Especially two gunmen as good as these killers were.

"We'll pick up their trail tomorrow," Bill promised Fire-away.

He reined his horse around and started back toward the workcamp.

Chapter Nine

Kristen McCoy breathed in deeply of the morning air, rejoicing in the fine weather. The world today reminded her of a newly emerged butterfly, shimmering and fragile and beautiful in the sun.

"Git up!" she called to her handsome new pair of bay horses, flicking the reins across their rumps.

Kristen's big wagon was back on the road again thanks to her nearest neighbors, Hiram and Dottie Kunkle. The Kunkles were a kindly, elderly couple who had lost three of their six children to smallpox. They had insisted on selling Kristen the team, on credit, until she could make a going concern of her new homestead.

The only way to do that, Kristen realized, was to grow and sell more fruit-tree seedlings. Lord, how this vast new country needed apple, peach, and cherry trees! To that end, she was visiting area farmers. So far, they had shown great enthusiasm for her pa's dream of starting fruit orchards here in Kansas.

Then, for a moment, thinking of Wild Bill Hickok, Kristen felt a little stab of guilt. After all, he had kindly given her forty dollars which was currently feeding her family. Perhaps she had been too quick to condemn him?

"Cameron!" Kristen snapped at the same perverse little imp who had twice challenged Hickok. "Don't be hitting your sisters!"

"I *ain't* hittin' 'em," the towhead sassed back. "They just keep running into my fist."

"Just 'cause papa never whaled you a good one," Kristen warned her little brother, "don't mean I won't."

"Whale a cat's tail," the little hellion sneered. "I'm a man, ain't no girl gunna make *me* cry."

"Why, you little brat! I'll tan your britches for you right now!"

But even as Kristen reined back and pushed forward on the hand brake, she noticed a hen pheasant suddenly whir up from a little stand of juniper just ahead—as if startled.

Maybe a fox spooked it, she thought. However, a moment later, a man astride a big sorrel moved out into the middle of the rutted lane.

The brakes squealed in protest when the big wagon lurched to a halt. The man sat in his saddle, picking his teeth with a twig. The smile he flashed at her failed to include his cold, detached eyes.

"Yes?" Kristen demanded. "What is it, sir?"

"It's *you*," Ansel Logan replied. "I mean, sugar, you are one fine-lookin' woman."

Something furtive and animal in his manner frightened Kristen. But it was not the McCoy way to surrender to fear.

"I shall always treasure that compliment in the locket of my heart," Kristen said scornfully. "Now please stand aside."

Kristen snapped the reins, but Logan quickly reached down and caught hold of the harness.

"Hot damn, sugar," he said. "Why'n't you try bein' nice to me? Did somebody steal your rattle when you was a baby?"

Kristen realized it was going to get ugly. She felt her knees go watery with fear.

"I don't know you," she informed the stranger with icy hauteur. "And I was not raised to tolerate strangers who get too familiar."

"Sweetheart, you got a voice like waltzing violins, know that? Damn fine titties, too."

Blood rushed into Kristen's face. Ansel saw the pulse suddenly throbbing in the arch of her slim throat. He wanted to kiss that throb—for starters.

By now Kristen's nostrils quivered with indignation. "You filthy hyena," she said with chilling contempt.

91

Ansel took in her thick, wheat-colored hair, her fine alabaster skin. Kristen felt a lump lodge in her throat when he threw the twig away and slid the pistol from his hand-tooled holster.

"Are you going to shoot us, big man?" she demanded. "An unarmed woman and three kids?"

"Naw. No shooting, sugar. I'm damned if I'll damage quality goods like you unless I hafta."

Kristen shrank back on the seat when Logan inserted the cold, hard muzzle of his six-shooter into the top of her dress. One quick downward tug, and he had exposed her thin chemise. Two plum-colored circles dinted the fine fabric where her heavy nipples pressed against it.

"*Mighty* fine titties," Logan said, having trouble with his breathing now. "Just climb in the back there, hon, and lay down. We're gonna make us some *fine* whoopee."

Logan was too distracted to care that little Cameron had vaulted over the side into the lane and picked up a rock.

"You'll have to kill me," Kristen assured him.

"That's your choice, sugar britches. Long as it's still warm for me," Logan replied, thumbing back the hammer of his Colt.

Cameron threw the rock with all his young might. It smacked Logan in the right temple. He loosed a grunt of pain, his eyes suddenly losing their focus.

The blow didn't knock him out, but managed to stun him.

"Get in the wagon!" Kristen ordered her brother, acting quickly. She pushed at Logan with all her strength, knocking him out of his saddle and down beside the lane.

"G'wan!" Kristen shouted, standing up on the high seat and fetching the sorrel a good kick in the shoulder. It reared back once, then took off to the east.

"Gee up!" Kristen shouted at her own team, grabbing the whip from its socket to lash the horses. She felt her heart pounding in her throat.

"You stinking son of a bitch!" Cameron shouted back toward the man. This time, a grateful Kristen didn't swat her gutsy little brother for cussing.

Like all survivors on the frontier, Wild Bill Hickok had a sixth sense attuned to catastrophe. Sometimes, however, danger crept up on a man unexpectedly.

After the murder of Wilson, several frightened workmen had drawn their pay and quit. The Kansas-Pacific was already seriously short-handed thanks to the sniper; they had no choice but to suspend work temporarily until they could hire on new workers.

Hickok, disgusted with himself at his lack of progress in this case, had no good choice but to return to Abilene for the time being.

With his altered appearance, and grimy work clothes, Bill felt safe visiting the Alamo Saloon for a real poker game. On their first night back in town, he led Josh toward the four baize-top tables at the rear of the saloon, reserved for serious cardplayers.

Before long, Bill was invited to play by a middle-aged gent named Gladstone. He was a harmless, good-natured fellow with a crest of frizzled gray hair and the booming, hollow brashness of a drummer. But before long, the three men were joined by another player who immediately set Josh's nerves on edge. He had a Latin look, Josh thought—pig Latin.

He introduced himself as Jay Hobert of Pine Bluff, Arkansas. Josh disliked him from the get go. Hobert had a lipless smile and a small, shrewd head like a wet rodent. His nose humped in the middle from an old break. As Josh described him later in an article for the *New York Herald*: "He had the sullen, withdrawn contempt of men destined to die on sawdust-covered floors."

At first, however, things went smoothly enough. Josh, too broke to afford the one-dollar ante, served as dealer. The men stuck mostly to five-card draw. Hobert stayed quiet, but Josh noticed he was slugging back shots of rye whiskey like it was sasparilla.

It soon became clear that Bill was riding a streak tonight. He took four hands out of five, the coins rapidly stacking up in front of him.

"Damn, O'Brien," Hobert remarked as Bill scooped in yet another pot. "For a man dressed in filthy working togs, you sure's hell know your way around a poker deck."

Despite the dark hint here, Bill maintained his usual Olympian detachment.

"Luck of the draw," he replied politely. But Josh could tell that Bill's glacial calmness cankered at Hobert.

Trying to head off trouble, Gladstone said heartily, "Well, Mr. Hobert. What brings you to Abilene, sir? Cattle business?"

Hobert knocked back another slug of coffin varnish.

"The bounty-huntin' business, friend," he replied. "Scuttlebutt has it that Bill Hickok is in these parts. That dandy bastard is worth ten thousand dollars dead, and I mean to help him get his life over quick."

Josh felt a moment of paralyzing stupefaction. Bill, however, flashed a little grin.

"Wake up," Bill chided Josh. "Deal the hand, kid."

Hobert had been waiting for a chance. Now he seized it.

"Why'n't you leave the kid alone?" he demanded belligerently. "Pick on somebody that's got his growth."

Bill shrugged it off, knowing Hobert was talking through whiskey fumes. But when Hickok took the next two hands, Hobert suddenly slammed his whiskey bottle to the table so hard that it knocked over Bill's neat stacks of coins.

"You damn popinjay!" Hobert exploded. He tried to look tough by breathing through his teeth. "You're markin' 'em damn cards with your cigar ashes!"

No hint this time. Hobert spoke loudly enough for everyone else to hear him. The Alamo suddenly went ominously still and quiet except for chairs scraping backward as men cleared a hole for whatever was surely coming.

"I'm not looking for any trouble," Bill told the blowhard quietly.

Hobert's lipless mouth was set like a trap. "*Course* you ain't, card cheat. You ain't got the stones for it, you yellow-bellied, white-livered, milk-kneed sonofabitch!"

"You flap your mouth too much," Bill said evenly.

"Mister, I ain't one for skating around the edges. So I'll just put it to you plain: I don't like your goddamn face."

"That works out real handy, then," Bill said. "Because it's not for sale."

Almost everyone in the saloon laughed at this retort except Hobert. Bill had once told Josh that danger showed in the lower half of a man's face, and that was the part Hickok watched now.

Hobert made a big production out of scraping back his chair and standing up. "That's enough damn palaver, O'Brien. You oughtn't to've pushed it. Now make your play."

"With what?" Bill replied. "I'm not armed."

Hobert sneered. "Don't surprise me none. If you ever shot a man, it'd be in the back."

A drunk cowboy, eager to liven things up with some gunplay, unbuckled his gunbelt and placed the rig on the table near Bill. "There's six beans in the wheel," he said.

"That's called a gun," Hobert told Bill. "A *man* wears one all the time. Strap it on, mouthpiece."

"Don't think I will," Bill told him, and Josh alone knew why: Hickok was not eager to reveal his true identity, not in this den of potential killers. Not even to kill low-life pond scum like Hobert. Too, it would ruin Bill's useful cover as Liam O'Brien.

"It's past choosin', mister! Either you strap on that iron, or I'll cut you down where you sit!"

Trapped, Bill shrugged, stood up, and did as told. "I'll give it a try," he said uncertainly. "Who goes first? Do we draw straws?"

This drew a contemptuous laugh throughout the saloon. Hobert snorted.

"I won't go for my gun until you make your play," the tough assured him. "Ladies first."

Bill nodded as if that sounded fair to him. Josh and Gladstone drew out of the line of fire.

Josh saw Bill discreetly glance into the chamber, making sure there was a bullet under the

97

hammer. He strapped on the belt, fumbling a bit as if unused to the task.

"Well?" Hobert demanded. "The hell you waitin' on, Christmas? You damned coward, I'll . . . *Jee*-zus!"

One moment Hickok's hand dangled two feet from the holster; the next, a six-shooter filled his fist with steel-blue authority. No one saw any movement—not even a blur.

"Just a dry run," Bill apologized politely. He holstered the weapon again. "You ready now?"

"Jeezus," Hobert said again, scared sober now. He ran the tip of his tongue over his lips. "I—uhh, that is to say, I'm—well, now that I think on it, Mister O'Brien, mayhap I was a mite quick to rise up on my hind legs. I just *thought* I saw a marked card, is all."

"Mistakes happen," Bill conceded.

"Why, Christ!" said the bar dog suddenly, leaning over the deal counter to stare closer at Bill. "Ain't that Bill Hickok?"

"Bernie," said another man, "you been grazing locoweed? If that was Bill Hickok, Mister Hobert would already be shoveling coal in hell. It ain't Hickok's way to clear his holster without shooting."

" 'Sides," someone else tossed in, "Hickok wouldn't be caught dead in them filthy workin' rags—no offense, O'Brien. Hickok's a prissy when it comes to clothes, almost womanish."

"That's right," Josh said, biting his lip to keep from laughing as Bill frowned. "Wild Bill is a bit of a peacock."

"Does this mean I win the gunfight?" Bill said uncertainly, and the room exploded in laughter.

Chapter Ten

"Lads!" shouted Taffy Blackford. "An honest pagan is better than a bad Catholic! And by the Lord Harry, *I'm* an honest pagan! I live on bachelor's fare: bread and cheese and kisses, aye!"

The men riding on the railroad flatcar exploded with laughter at Blackford's foolish antics. Taffy was entertaining and likable, a redheaded Welshman full of youthful vitality. Men like Taffy were welcome on railroad labor crews. They made a long work shift pass quicker and the time off more enjoyable.

The birds were still celebrating sunup when the work train—crowded with new hirelings—pulled out of Abilene at the first dull, leaden light of dawn. By now it had turned into a fine day, cool and clear, the sky a deep, bottomless blue like a gas flame.

Nonetheless, Josh noticed how Wild Bill—still Liam O'Brien to their fellow workers—kept his worried eyes focused in the distance. These men were vulnerable because work trains were made up of just a locomotive and tender, one boxcar for animals, and an open flatcar for the men. And some of the men were drunk as Davy's saw.

"Lads!" Taffy called out. "Always top an ugly woman in the dark. For you see, a nod is as good as a wink to a blind horse!"

More laughter, whistles, and cheers. A bottle of cheap mash made the rounds. Even Josh took a nip to offset the morning chill.

"It just doesn't seem right," Josh remarked to Bill, "that two men can stop an entire railroad."

"Grass can push a stone over," Bill reminded him. "It just needs time, is all."

Bill was under increasing pressure from Pinkerton. The Kansas-Pacific, delayed almost two months now by the sniper, was on the verge of giving this new line up as a bad job.

"Drink life to the lees, boys!" Taffy roared out. "Eat the whole of the meat and none of the parsley! Give over fretting, stout lads! There's whiskey to be drunk, women to be had, songs to be sung!"

The train rumbled on toward end-of-track, through night-frosted meadows of timothy and clover. As the day warmed up, Josh could see the first mud daubers active in the puddles beside the tracks.

Bill's steady, gunmetal gaze never left the distant terrain.

"Think they're out there this early?" Josh asked him.

Wild Bill lifted one shoulder. "How long is a piece of string? Damned if I know."

Taffy was still at it. He accepted the bottle from another man and hoisted it high in a toast.

"More power to your elbow, lads!"

Taffy drank a sweeping-deep slug.

"Aye, *that's* medicine! Boys, these temperance biddies say them who *drink* whiskey will *think* whiskey! But that's cow plop! I say them who drink water will *think* water!"

Everyone laughed, including Josh and Bill.

"He's a caution," Josh said.

"His mouth runs like a whipperwill's ass," Bill replied. "But the fellow is entertaining. And clowns like him are generally hard workers, too."

And so it went as the work train rolled closer to end-of-track. About fifteen minutes from their destination, Josh saw Bill abruptly stiffen like a hound on point.

Later, when it was too late, Bill would explain to Josh that he had glimpsed a brief glint—as if a rifle scope had momentarily reflected sunlight.

"Everybody cover down!" Wild Bill roared out. "Cover down *now,* damnit!"

But no one heeded his warning in time. O'Brien was an aloof stranger to them; who the hell was *he* to give orders? Besides, many of the men were drunk and failed to heed the urgency in his tone.

Josh heard a *thuck* sound like a rock punching into mud. The man next to him keeled over backwards, blood blossoming from his chest.

Thuck! A second man tumbled off the flatcar and hit the ground like a parcel of bouncing rags.

Thuck! And Taffy Blackford grunted hard when his breastbone shattered.

The three bullets arrived only a second or two apart. Because of the clattering noise of the train, no one ever heard the gunshots. The frightened men finally pressed down as flat as possible. With good targets thus eliminated, the sniping ended, at least for now.

Nonetheless, Wild Bill rushed forward, scrambled over the tender, and told the engineer to fire his boilers to full pressure. The faster they could roll, the quicker they'd be out of effective range.

Two men, Josh realized, were already stone dead. And Taffy Blackford lay at death's threshold by the time Bill made it back.

"Don't look so sad, boys," the game Welshman managed to say, blood and spittle frothing pink on his lips. "The journey . . . the journey is long, but this world isn't the end. Not on your Nellie! It's . . . it's just a station stop."

Josh, his face pale as moonstone, watched death shudders seize the redhead.

"I only joked about b-b-being a pa-pagan," he managed. "I'll suh-suh-see you all in pa-paradise!"

The final moments were gut-wrenching for all who witnessed it. Taffy choked in his own blood and called pitifully for his mother. Then, with a final violent shudder, his head rolled to one side, and he gave up the ghost.

The death stunned every man to silence, including Bill. Josh had read a hundred deaths described in dime novels, but never one like this. It left him feeling as if he'd been drop-kicked in the belly.

"It's 'Bama Jones," Wild Bill said, as if speaking to convince himself. Josh had never seen Bill look as helpless, angry, and frustrated as he did right now.

"Damnit, kid," Bill added. "I'm quitting the Pinkerton Agency."

But Bill took one last, long look at the dead Welshman. Then he added in a tone of willful determination, "*After* I air out that scum-sucking Jones."

Not surprisingly, the work train returned—after dark—to Abilene with many of the new workers onboard. Most had seen enough and had quit the same day. But Wild Bill and Josh sprang their horses from the boxcar and remained behind. For Hickok had decided on a nighttime tracking mission.

"Darkness," he informed Josh, "is the only damn defense we have against shooters like 'Bama. Even that may not be enough. Here, kid. Gop some of this on your face."

Josh followed Bill's lead and smeared his face with mud to cut reflection.

"I'm going to dog those bastards from now on," Bill vowed. "Stay on them like ugly on a buzzard. They've had it too easy, just plinking at targets of opportunity. Let's see if they can eat what they dish out."

"My editor thinks this is a great story," Josh said. "Newspaper circulation is up since I started covering you. But after what I saw today, I'd rather sling hash for a cow outfit."

"You were hungry for glory," Bill reminded him, "when you first looked me up in Denver. Sounds like you've got a belly full of it now."

"Yeah," Josh agreed. "No glory in it. Just cold-blooded murder."

It didn't take long, searching under the light of a star-spangled sky, to find the exact spot where 'Bama and his companion had set up their deadly ambush camp atop a low rise.

A blind man could have followed the ruts of the big bone wagon they'd left in. It bore due south, away from the KP tracks.

"Following them ain't the hard work," Bill commented. "Getting close to them is the tricky part. Well, at least we seem to've lost Calamity Jane for a while. That's almost worth getting killed for."

On and on the two men trekked while the stars thickened and the moon crept toward its zenith. They kept their horses to a canter, which Bill favored because they made good time but spared the animals.

Another hour passed. They rode into a low, marshy swale, the horse's hooves making slow sucking noises. As they rode out and crested a low ridgeline, Bill suddenly reined in.

"Jesus! Watch your skyline," Bill warned tensely, swinging out of the saddle. "There they are. Back the horses up."

The two men retreated back behind the ridge and hobbled their mounts foreleg to rear with strips of rawhide.

"We go in slow," Bill told Josh. "It looks deserted, but that could be a lure. Stay well behind me, stay low, and only move when I give the high sign. Stop when I signal. Kid, for Christ sakes, don't play the hero. Don't forget that 'Bama's got a trick-shooter with him. These boys don't throw lead, they *aim* it."

Josh nodded, trying to ignore the ball of ice in his belly. Bill palmed both cylinders to check his loads. Then he went back over the ridge, low-crawling this time.

Josh kept Bill's boot heels in sight, crawling only when Bill waved him on. Ants and mosquitoes bit at Josh's skin, gnats plagued his eyes to tears. Each yard forward made Josh recall how this might be a trick—how they might be in a gun sight even now.

He poured sweat, and the cold night wind cooled him to chills. Finally Bill waved him off, and Josh waited for all hell to break loose as Bill moved on in. The bone wagon loomed big in the moonlight, the oxen tethered nearby and taking off the grass.

Finally, after an interminable wait, Josh heard Bill cuss out loud.

"Well, shit! C'mon in, Longfellow. They've flown the coop."

The big wagon, bones gleaming a dull white in the bed, had been deserted. The ashes of a small campfire still gave scant heat, but no light. Bill estimated the two men had left perhaps two to three hours ago.

"There's two of them, all right," he confirmed, quickly reading the signs. "You can see where they cut two horses loose from the wagon's tailgate. And look—they rode due east. Straight toward Abilene."

"Look," Josh said, pointing toward the wagon seat. "They left something."

It was a leather musette bag, tied closed with a rawhide whang. Bill untied it, reached inside, then cursed violently and leaped backward, almost knocking Josh down. Josh saw the vicious fangs of a three-foot-long rattlesnake sink deep into Bill's right hand! The reptile was so close Josh could clearly see the green spackles on its back.

Bill drew his left-side Colt, shot the snake off his hand, and had his case knife out in seconds.

"Bastards bamboozled me good, kid," he said, grimacing in pain. "Old Indian trick. See how they cut the rattle off?"

"Jesus," Josh said. "Jesus, Bill! What should I do?"

But Hickok remained calm and worked quickly. Never flinching, he cut two deep slices in a cross shape over the fang marks. Then Bill sucked and spit several times, spewing the venomous blood from his mouth.

When Josh almost got sick to his stomach and had to sit down, Hickok grinned at him in the moonlight. He spit more blood and poison out. Then he said, "Just be glad it didn't bite me on the ass, kid, or *you'd* be doing this for me."

Bill took the bottle of Old Taylor from a saddle pocket, washed out the wound, then ripped a strip from his shirt and bound it.

"I might run a fever," he explained, "but I got most of the venom out in time. I could taste that nasty crap."

Bill stared in the direction of Abilene, his face pensive.

"That town's an old whore that keeps calling me back," he said softly. "And she definitely means to kill me."

Bill shook off his mood and walked close to the team, shooting each ox in the head. Then he said briskly, "C'mon, kid. Let's torch that damn wagon.

At least we'll destroy their cover and make it harder for them to hide."

"Yeah, but then what?"

"Whad'ja think? We dust our hocks back to Abilene and hunt those two dry gulchers out, that's what. I want them dead, kid. Dead as last Christmas."

Chapter Eleven

"How's 'at, boys?" Ansel Logan demanded, slapping down a stack of freshly printed handbills onto the raw-wood bar of the Alamo Saloon. "Ol' Hickok flummoxed everybody at first. But he won't be laughing up his sleeve for long."

'Bama Jones and the bounty hunter named Jay Hobert each picked up one of the flyers.

NOTICE!!! TO ALL WHO WOULD LIKE TO BE $10,000 RICHER!!! JAMES BUTLER "WILD BILL" HICKOK IS PRESENTLY IN THE ABILENE AREA, MINUS HIS LONG HAIR AND MUSTACHE.

"Christ Jesus!"

Hobert knuckled his shot glass aside and aimed a popeyed stare at the sketch of Hickok. It was a good likeness made from a popular portrait of him in *Harper's Weekly*. But it left off the distinctive long hair and mustache.

"You sure this is Hickok?" Hobert demanded.

"Sure as the Lord made Moses," Logan replied. " 'Bama recognized him this morning on the work train."

"Well, I'll go to hell," Hobert said wonderingly. "I played poker with that son of a bitch yestiddy! I never once twigged his game."

"Hickok," 'Bama declared, his mouth full of boiled egg, "is a fox-eared bastard, all right. Shiftier than a creased buck."

"Well, give over fretting, porky," Logan said. "These handbills will settle his hash. I'm posting 'em all over Abilene. He'll wish he'd died as a child."

"Bill Goddamn Hickok," Hobert repeated, still staring at the black-ink likeness. "Ten thousand dollars, three feet away from me all night, and me just sittin' on my prat."

Hobert filled his glass with rye, picked it up between thumb and forefinger, and tossed it back. He slammed the glass back down. His eyes went dark with brooding.

"Can you hold off a bit on postin' them notices?" he asked.

Logan shook his head. "Sorry. First come, best served."

"Well, then, you can post all the notices you please," Hobert told his two new drinking companions. "But *I* mean to put paid to it first."

111

"Have at it," Logan said. "I could use the money myself. But mainly I just want the bastard cold—cold as a fish on ice, if you take my drift."

Logan was too preoccupied with other matters to care about competing for the first shot at Hickok. He was already making plenty from the Santa Fe Railroad. And Kristen McCoy's pure white skin had become an obsession with him since that damned guttersnipe brother of hers had laid Logan's skull open with a rock. The tender swelling beside his ear had just begun to recede.

But Logan didn't scare off that easy. Not where fine woman flesh like the McCoy gal was the prize.

'Bama finished his sixth boiled egg, then tied into a bowl of pickled pig's feet.

"Finish feedin' your face," Logan told the sniper. "Then we'll plaster up these notices. Hickok could be coming back any time now. He weren't on the work train when it come back to town. I checked."

"In that case," Hobert said, flipping a silver dollar onto the bar to cover four drinks, "I'll be heading outside to take up a good position. The man who means to plug Hickok first will have to make his play quick."

The word about Bill Hickok's new disguise spread through Abilene like grease through a goose. Bill and Josh, exhausted after their night scout west of town, emerged from the hotel about an hour before sundown.

Immediately, they spotted one of the handbills on the front of the mercantile store.

"*Ho*-ly smoke!" Josh exclaimed. "There must be a hundred of 'em up!"

But Wild Bill merely shrugged, admiring the likeness.

"Jesus, I'm a handsome man," he complimented himself.

"Want me to rip 'em down?"

Bill shook his head. "Nah, don't bother. Won't help now."

Bill stuck a cheroot in his teeth, fired a match to life with his thumbnail, and leaned into the flame. Shading his eyes from the sun, Bill studied the street.

"Looks calm," he remarked. "But then, so does a graveyard."

Josh felt sweat oozing out from under his hatband. He was still bone tired, and his mouth felt as dry and stale as the last cracker in the barrel. Nervously, he watched two cowboys pull in at the Alamo. They lit down and wrapped their reins around the tie rail. Otherwise, Texas Street looked calm and empty.

"Shouldn't we at least head for the shadows?" he suggested.

Bill grinned at him. "S'matter, kid? 'Fraid the bullet might drift? Let's head over to the Western Union. It's just about to close."

Another express courier had arrived from Pinkerton. Bill's suggestion had paid off. Pinkerton monitored telegraphic messages stored on the trunkline drum, or perforation-storage unit, that originated in Abilene. Although they were written in some kind of keyword code Pinkerton couldn't decipher, it was clear that regular reports were being sent to important officials of the Santa Fe Railroad.

"All that is good to know," Bill had commented. "It confirms who's bankrolling the killing around here. And now we know some of the telegraphers are on the payroll. But it doesn't eliminate the real problem of 'Bama Jones, or tell us who his trick-shooting companion is."

Josh tried to quell his nervous stomach as the two men strolled across the street. Boot heels thudding on the boardwalk, they aimed for the telegraph office.

"Hang around out here, Longfellow," Bill said. "Keep a weather eye out."

A bell tinkled as Bill entered the little cubbyhole office. The bald-headed clerk in sleeve garters and green eyeshades glanced up as Bill entered.

"You just made it, mister," he said. "I'm about to close up shop."

Bill wore both ivory-grip Colts hidden under a cloth work coat. In a heartbeat, each fist was filled with iron. The clerk's Adam's apple bobbed up and down.

114

"No," Bill corrected him. "*I'm* about to close up shop. Permanently. Unless you tell me who's paying you to send secret reports to the Santa Fe Railroad."

"Muh-muh-mister, I don't know what in Suh-Suh-Sam Hill you're talking about! Honest to Christ I don't! I—"

Bill thumbed back both hammers. The sound was ominously loud in that small office.

"Usually," Bill explained, "I shoot first and ask questions later. In your case I've made an exception. But not for long. Now try again."

The telegrapher had to grab the counter when his knees gave out. But he knew who was talking and precisely what he meant.

"The guh-guh-gentleman's name is Ansel Luh-Luh-Logan," he replied as promptly as he could.

The sound of the name struck Bill almost like a slap to the face. Yet he wondered why he didn't think of Logan sooner. Bill, who had toured briefly with Colonel Cody's Wild West Show, knew Ansel Logan well enough to respect—and fear—the man's superb marksmanship.

"Where's he staying?" Bill pressed.

"Muh-muh-mister, my hand to God! I couldn't tell you that."

Bill believed him. The man was too timid to hold back any information. Hickok returned to the boardwalk and reported this new fact to Josh.

"So who or what is Ansel Logan?" the young reporter demanded.

"He can sight into a mirror," Bill replied, "and aiming over his shoulder, shoot a shot glass off a bulldog's head at forty paces. I've seen him do it. If he hadn't tried to rape every girl in Bill Cody's troupe, he'd still be Buffalo Bill's star shooter. But Cody's a gentleman, and he won't stand for that rough tomcatting."

Even as he spoke, Hickok's fathomless eyes scoured Abilene.

"Well, day's closing in," he told Josh. "Let's eat. My backbone's rubbing against my ribs."

From necessity, it was Hickok's habit to study every possible clue before he stepped into a street. Especially now, with his face plastered all over town. Even as he took his first step off the board-walk, Bill caught a shadow in the corner of his vision: a shadow that didn't belong where it was.

Josh had not yet stepped into the street.

"Freeze right there," Bill told the kid quietly.

The westering sun threw the slanted shadow of a man into the middle of Texas Street—a man crouching up on top the building beside the Western Union office.

Wild Bill calculated his chances quickly. He could easily hop back up onto the boardwalk, out of the line of fire. But maybe the best play now, with those handbills all over town, was to send out a strong warning to all would-be assassins.

The trick part, Hickok realized, was to move far enough into the street to give himself a line of fire. But that also meant the risk of giving the gunman first shot.

Bill took one step, then another. Just as he finished the third step he drew steel, whirled, fell to one side, and fired exactly when the gunman did.

The mystery shooter had a dead aim. But Bill saved his own life by falling at a slant. The slug whizzed past his head with the sound of an angry hornet, so close Bill felt heat lick his ear.

The gunman above wasn't so lucky. Bill's slug caught him high in the chest. He threw both arms out to the heavens like a priest in the pulpit. Then he crashed into the low, flimsy false front and took a piece of it with him when he crashed down onto the boardwalk, barely missing Josh.

"*Jump*-ing Jehoshaphat!" the scribe exclaimed.

The shots started to draw a crowd. Keeping a wary eye on them, Bill said, "Check him, kid. It's Hobert, I see."

Josh knew that Bill was worried, as usual, about possum players. Once, a "dead man" had almost planted a slug in his back while Bill crossed the battlefield at Second Bull Run.

Josh knelt and felt Hobert's neck for a pulse.

"Dead," he pronounced. "If the bullet didn't kill him, the broken neck did."

Bill nodded, still watching the crowd. Neither 'Bama Jones nor Ansel Logan were among them.

"Anybody else wants to air out Wild Bill Hickok," he said in his mild way, "is welcome to

117

try. Anybody can get lucky, and hell, I have to die once, now don't I?"

Everyone stared at Hobert's wide-open, death-surprised eyes. But no one answered Bill's question. And as Josh wrote later in his next dispatch for the *New York Herald*: "What, really, could anyone say?"

Chapter Twelve

Everywhere she went now, Kristen McCoy was armed for trouble.

She had located, and thoroughly cleaned, her pa's trusty old Winchester "Yellow Boy" rifle, so called for its bright brass barrel. Now it lay on the board seat beside her with a round under the hammer.

"Hee-*yahh!*" she called to her team of bays, stepping up the pace as she returned to her new homestead a few miles north of Abilene.

Kristen had just finished selling a dozen fruit-tree seedlings to a local farmer. She had explained to him how easy it was to spread manure evenly through the new orchards. Soon enough, plums, peaches, and apples would flourish among the wheat and corn fields of Kansas.

Lord, but her pa would be so proud of her for carrying on his work. Kristen recalled how lovingly her father had taken his seedlings to bed with him in winter to keep them warm. The newspapers these days were full of sensational stories about men like Wild Bill Hickok, Wyatt Earp, and John Wesley Hardin. But it was quiet, visionary men like her pa whose hard work was turning this barren New World into a Garden of Eden.

Kristen, lost deep in her thoughts, suddenly realized that a lone rider was approaching her from behind.

Immediately her temples began to pulse with nervous blood. Kristen recalled that pale stranger with those dead, glass-button eyes.

This man could be him, returning to rape her! And he was approaching at a fast canter.

"Git!" she shouted to her bays, flicking the sisal whip across their rumps. "Git! Git *up* there, damnit!"

But the moment she began moving faster, the rider pushed his mount to a full gallop.

By the time Kristen thought to study the horse's markings, too much dust obscured it. Kristen fought down her fear and took up the Winchester, cocking it. Her pa had given her lessons and turned her into a fair-to-middling marksman.

She slewed around in the high seat and settled the butt plate into her shoulder socket. The recoil kicked into her shoulder and almost made her tumble off the seat.

But it was a good shot. The man's black, broad-brimmed hat sailed off. With an amazingly deft reaction, he reached out and caught it.

Now Kristen realized: This man wasn't the same one who'd tried to molest her. His hair was shorter, lighter, and less coarse. And he had a handsome, vaguely familiar face.

"Whoa!" she called out to her team, pulling back on the reins. But Kristen took no chances—she jacked another round into the chamber and kept Yellow Boy aimed at the man as he rode up.

"Jesus, dumpling," the handsome stranger greeted her. "Why'n't you lower that fire stick a mite? You already let daylight into my favorite hat."

"It's you!" Kristen finally recognized Hickok without his curls and facial hair. She lowered the rifle and added, "You look better without all that foppish hair. But at first I mistook you for the two-legged weasel who tried to . . . attack me a few days back."

"Black hair and a lopsided mouth?" Bill asked her. "Snake-eyed, likes to chew on twigs?"

Kristen nodded. "You know him?"

"I know him, and I mean to kill him. So far, though, I've got nothing but his dust. You just keep on giving him the slip, hear? That one's wearing the no-good label."

"He comes pesticatin' around me again," Kristen vowed, "he'll be wearing lead in his belly."

"Don't bury him too quick," Bill warned. "He's the same hombre you watched kill those six soldiers."

Kristen paled at this intelligence, momentarily speechless. Bill took a long, appreciative look at the striking blonde. Young, but a full-grown woman with a woman's knowledge in her eyes. She wore a simple white shirtwaist tucked into frayed and faded blue jeans. Her hair hung in two long braids tied with white ribbons in front of each shoulder.

Sure as hell, she's pretty and shapely, Bill thought. But it wasn't just the color and lines that gave value to the best horses *or* women. It was a mysterious quality the Spanish called *brio escondido*, "the hidden vigor." And Kristen McCoy was brimming over with it.

"Like what you're staring at?" she demanded.

"No misdoubting that. Just wish I could see more than I do."

Instead of taking offense, Kristen surprised him with a smile.

"I like the way you're honest without insulting me. You're different that way. My pa used to say there's some men who bees won't sting. You ever been stung, Mr. Hickok?"

Bill grinned, liking the turn this trail was taking. "Never by bee, wasp, or hornet," he admitted.

He held up his injured hand. "But rattlesnakes like to chew on me."

"Aww," she cooed. "Shall Krissy kiss it and make it all better?" she teased him.

Bill grinned and nudged Fire-away in even closer.

"Actually," he told her, "you know what? That damn snake bit me right on the mouth, too. Hurts like hell."

"Poor baby!" Kristen was losing no time making up for her earlier coldness toward him. "Let's see if I can ease your pain."

Her full, heart-shaped lips parted slightly as Bill leaned forward to kiss them. But at the first pleasurable contact, a pistol barked nearby.

Bill flinched, and Kristen cried out in fright.

"Christ on a crutch!" Bill exclaimed as the precisely aimed bullet blew the high heel off his left boot.

"Bill Hickok, damn your handsome bones to hell! I don't care how many fillies you keep in your stable. But *don't* by God be swappin' spit with 'em in front of me!"

"Well, damnit, Jane! In front of you? You dog me like my shadow. Always hemming me."

"You don't bawl about it when I save your bacon! I *got* to trail you, Bill, on account we got us a destiny, you randy-pantsed Lothario! A shared destiny, only you ain't man enough to

123

accept your half of it yet. I'm just keepin' you alive until you see the light."

"Jane," Bill pleaded, knowing it was useless. "I ain't in danger now! That old Mexer gal down in El Paso that told you all that 'destiny' hogwash don't know her ass from her elbow."

"Don't matter. She knows my palm."

By now Kristen had recovered from her fright. She stared—gaping in pure astonishment—at this stout, homely young woman dressed in man's clothing. Only Jane's immaculate gray Stetson passed muster.

"Who or what is that?" she demanded, but low so Jane couldn't hear.

"That," Bill replied grimly, "is my cross to bear through this life."

"You're full of it, Bill," Calamity Jane roared back. "That old gal in El Paso previsions the future! She's a witch, got the Third Eye."

Bill shook his head in disgusted frustration. Once Jane grabbed hold of a notion, there was no shaking her loose from it.

"You take care, Miss McCoy," Bill said with exaggerated formality, lifting his hat. He wheeled his mount around and rode back toward Abilene.

"You know where I live," she called behind him. "Don't let Cameron scare you off; he likes you now."

"That *bruja*," Jane roared at Bill as he retreated, "also said to tell you, beware the Number 10 Saloon in Deadwood! And she said, beware the dead man's hand! Aces and eights will get you kilt, Bill!"

But Hickok just waved her off in disgust and kept riding.

"Good news, bo," 'Bama Jones told Ansel Logan in his slow southern drawl. "Word in town has it that the Kansas-Pacific will make only one more try at building that spur line. We plant another surveyor; we win the battle."

"Harken and heed, porky," Logan replied. "Don't be listening to Dame Rumor. You heard what Perry told us. Hickok and Pinkerton have traced the telegrams back to big nabobs with the Santa Fe line. That ain't all. Jay Hobert is dead, and our wagon and team are ruint. You call that 'winning,' you ignorant cracker? Hickok is still plenty dangersome. And he's hot on our trail."

While he spoke, Logan thumbed rounds into his big, steel-framed Smith & Wesson. The two men shared the big backyard of a local boarding-house for drifters called Ma Ketchum's Bunkhouse. A big, sagging barn and a row of rickety outhouses surrounded the yard on two sides. Along the third side of the yard, several horses drank from a water trough made by sawing a barrel into halves.

"What's got your teeth on edge?" 'Bama demanded, speaking around a mouthful of Ma Ketchum's cornbread. "Get over your peeve. Hickok ain't slowed us yet."

Logan was indeed feeling cross today. Earlier, he had ridden out to Kristen McCoy's place, but she was gone. So was that damned brat brother of hers, or Ansel would have hung the little hellhound up by his thumbs.

"All the matter with me," he replied, "is I need me a quick poke. But not on no damned whore."

'Bama shook his head in disgust. "Ain't you particular?" he said scornfully. "Hickok *will* send us up Salt River if you don't get that little blonde outta your head, bo."

Logan chewed on a twig and said nothing. He picked up a scrag end of broken board and handed it to 'Bama.

"Here, quit banging your gums," he told 'Bama, "and toss that up into the air high as you can."

'Bama shrugged out of his tight-fitting Rebel tunic. He grunted hard as he flung the scrap of wood overhead.

Ansel drew his gun so fast that 'Bama didn't even see it happen. Six times his muzzle spat fire, the board dancing and jerking across the sky as slugs riddled it.

'Bama walked over and picked it up off the ground, counting the holes.

"Jesus! Five out of six! That's holding and squeezing, all right."

Logan laughed. "Five my sweet aunt! Count 'em again, porky."

'Bama did. This time his big moon face went wide-eyed. One of the holes was slightly bigger than the others.

"God dawg! Two slugs went through the same bitty little hole!"

Logan reloaded, then holstered his gun.

"Nerve up, 'Bama. When it comes to bustin' caps, we ain't no clabber-lipped greenhorns. You're the rifle master, and I'm the king of the short irons. Hickok? He made his reputation from bedding actresses and bouncing drunk cowboys around. Won't be long now, we'll shoot that dandy to dog meat!"

Logan had just fallen silent and turned toward the house. Abruptly, a young boy in a straw hat tore around the front corner of the big boardinghouse. Logan and 'Bama paid the kid four bits a day, when they were in town, to keep watch on Texas Street.

"Hey, misters!" the kid shouted. "That man on the pretty roan is headed this way! He's hitching his horse out front now!"

Chapter Thirteen

Joshua emerged from the cafe on Texas Street just in time to spot Wild Bill.

The frontiersman had ridden out alone earlier to search for 'Bama Jones and Ansel Logan. Bill told Josh he suspected the two killers were probably holed up somewhere in town. But Bill didn't want to thoroughly search dangerous Abilene until under the cover of nightfall.

But like Josh, Bill had obviously heard the rapid shots behind Ma Ketchum's place. That must be why, Josh told himself, Wild Bill was taking a dangerous chance now as he hitched Fireaway in front of the boardinghouse.

Josh was taking a sack of sandwiches and pie to the hotel. He waved the bag now to get Bill's attention. Bill glanced rapidly around the near-empty street, then waved Josh over.

"I heard 'em, too," Josh said. "Six shots, real close together."

Bill nodded. "Gunshots in this town don't usually mean much. But that rapid, six-shot string used to be Ansel Logan's signature with Cody's show."

Bill looked calm enough, as he always did except when cornered by Calamity Jane. But Josh read trouble in his eyes, even a glint of uncertainty.

"Cover me from the corner of the house, kid," Bill said, still watching the street for trouble. "That back right corner, where the willow tree will give you good cover."

Josh eased out his old French pinfire and cocked it. Both men slipped into the shadowy side yard of Ma's Bunkhouse.

"Listen up, kid," Bill whispered. "This ain't Miles City; *don't* go for glory. No matter what happens to me, don't be a fool and go beyond that corner, hear? They'll cut you down faster than a finger snap."

Josh swallowed the lump in his throat. "You kidding? Don't worry, I've seen what these two can do, remember?"

"But then again. If you get a good bead on one of 'em," Bill added, "drill the son of a bitch. You got a good eye, for a Quaker's kid."

Bill fell silent as they reached the willow tree. For a long time, both men studied the apparently empty yard.

"They coulda gone in the house," Josh whispered.

Bill nodded. But his next remark reminded Josh of Hickok's remarkable powers of observation.

"I think they know I'm here, kid, and they're laying for me. Didja see that buck-toothed kid in the straw hat run around the house when I turned in?"

Josh nodded.

"I'd wager the kid was a sentry."

At this, Josh felt his calves go watery and remote.

"Then . . . where would they hide?" he whispered.

Before Bill could answer, something tipped over in the big barn at the far side of the yard. Josh heard a whispered curse.

"Answer your question?" Bill asked.

Josh watched Hickok remove his hat and set it near the house beside the sack of food. A hat, Bill once told him, gave a good target to shooters above you. Clearly, Bill was worried about that open loft above the big double doors of the barn.

Bill eased a Peacemaker out, checked his loads, then burst rapidly across fifteen feet of open yard to the cover of the next tree.

Nothing. Josh realized he was holding his breath, so he expelled it and commanded himself to take another.

Bill again moved suddenly and swiftly, like a snake striking at its prey. Thus he leapfrogged from tree to tree, covering perhaps half of the big yard.

Sweat poured out of Josh's hair now, and he sleeved it out of his eyes.

Bill was still alive. But now he faced a real dilemma—about forty feet of open yard, with no cover whatsoever until he reached the water trough to the right of the barn.

Josh flinched hard when Bill suddenly sent three shots into the loft to clear the line of fire as he started running. The lithe Hickok moved fast as a jack rabbit, but avoided a straight line so any shooters could not "lead" him with their aim. He fired the remaining three shells in his .44 as he zigzagged, again clearing the open loft.

He made it on raw guts, Josh told himself when Bill was about to dive behind the water trough. But Josh had rejoiced too early. Even as Bill started to slide behind cover, a single shot rang out from the barn.

Josh felt his face drain cold when Wild Bill grunted hard, blood blossoming from his chest!

It was Wild Bill's avoidance pattern that threw off Logan's aim just enough to save his life.

Nonetheless, the slug caught Bill high in his right pectoral muscle, near the shoulder, striking with the force of a sledgehammer.

Bill barely managed to cover down behind the trough, scattering some of the horses, before Logan sent several more slugs whining at him. Water spouted into the air as bullets chunked into the wooden trough. But Josh tossed two quick rounds at the loft, forcing Logan back to cover.

Bill still had six bullets in his left-side Peacemaker. But blood was pouring from his wound with alarming force.

Wincing at the hot, throbbing pain, Bill ripped a strip from his shirt. Then, holding it in place with his teeth, he tied off the wound as best he could for now.

While Bill was thus distracted, 'Bama Jones suddenly burst from the back of the barn. Moving with clumsy but amazing speed, the big southerner leaped onto a claybank milling with the rest of the horses.

Wedged awkwardly between fence and water trough, unable to clear his left holster, Bill had no shot at the rifle assassin.

Nor did Josh—just as 'Bama moved into the open, Ansel Logan suddenly swung down from the loft on a rope tied to a loading arm.

As he arced through the air, grinning in elation, Logan expertly dispersed his rounds between Josh's position and Bill's, pinning both men. Bill watched in helpless frustration as the killer literally swung onto the back of a big seventeen-hand sorrel and joined 'Bama in flight.

While the hollow drumbeat of escaping hooves filled Texas Street, the first windows banged open in Ma Ketchum's Bunkhouse. The violent shootout had alerted most of Abilene to trouble.

"You still alive, Bill?" Josh called out, already sprinting across the yard.

"I must be." Hickok groaned as he tried to sit up. "Death couldn't hurt this damn bad. *Damn* it, Longfellow! They gave us the slip again."

Josh helped him to his feet. Bill saw the first curious spectators starting to peek around the back corner of the house.

"Jesus," he said in a low voice, thinking of that reward on his head. "The pack senses wounded prey. Get me outta here, wouldja?"

Wincing with each painful effort, Bill drew his left-side gun and watched the gathering spectators.

"There's a doctor's office next to the mercantile," Josh suggested.

"No sawbones, kid. Not in this town. His scalpel might 'slip.' Get me back to your room at the hotel."

"But who'll take out that slug?" Josh protested.

"Doc Robinson, that's who."

"Me? Aww, man alive, Bill! I ain't never done it."

"I have. Time you learned if you want to sidekick with me. I'll guide you all the way. Just think what a story it'll give you."

"Yeah. But what if . . . well, what if I botch it and kill you?"

Bill wagged his Colt and a knot of men fell back, letting them pass.

"In that case," Bill replied weakly, for he was still losing copious amounts of blood, "make sure you collect that ten thousand dollars. And get me a fancy granite marker for my grave."

"Light that kerosene lamp," Bill instructed Josh, taking his second stiff belt of Old Taylor. "Keep the chimney off it so you can use the flame to heat your knife."

Bill took a third swallow of bourbon, numbing his body for the ordeal ahead.

He lay on Josh's narrow bed, still holding a Colt in his left hand. The door was locked and a chair wedged under it.

"We got nothing but their dust again," Bill told Josh. "But now we've routed them out. We've got them on the run. They can't come back to town, and we've ruined their cover as bone scavengers. Ahh—*damn* that hurts!"

Bill sucked in a hissing breath as Josh gingerly pulled the blood-soaked cloth from his wound.

"Now what?" the kid said nervously. He stared in grim fascination at the ugly, puckered flesh surrounding the wound.

"Pour some whiskey in it," Bill told him. "That's it, slop it in there good. Then heat the knife."

"How hot?"

"Till it glows red, you young idiot."

Bill kept an eye on the room's only window.

"We've got 'em on the run," Bill repeated. "But we have to track them down before they can kill another railroad employee."

But Josh was too nervous to listen to any of this.

"Knife's glowing," he reported. "Now what?"

"Whad'ja think? Dig that slug out, that's what. Work quick, kid. Do it once, and do it fast. First thing you do is probe with the tip of the knife until you feel it contact the slug. Soon's you locate it, cut straight down to it."

Josh caught his lower lip between his teeth. Gingerly, he poked the heated tip of the knife into the bullet hole.

"Jesus God, kid!" Hickok snapped impatiently. "You ain't carving jade! Cut the son of a bitch out, wouldja? Just—oh, *Christ!* Goddamnit, that hurts! That's the boy, just cut it loose—*yowch!*"

"Oh, man, there's so much blood," Josh wailed, but the plucky city boy did as ordered, working quickly and efficiently. When the red-hot blade cut deep into meat and tissue, Bill had to cram his leather belt between his teeth and bite down hard.

"I see it!" Josh exclaimed. "I see it! *There!*"

Triumphantly, the reporter held the flattened slug out between thumb and forefinger. Bill, awash on a sea of pain, barely nodded.

"Now what?" Josh demanded.

"Now comes the fun part. Heat your blade again," Bill said weakly. "You've got to cauterize the wound or it'll pus up."

Bill took another hit of Old Taylor while Josh heated the knife to a red glow again. The kid almost gagged at the bitter stink of scorched flesh when he laid the blade against Bill's wound, searing the ragged edges together.

"God kiss me!"

Bill's body bent like a drawn bow. Then his Colt .44 tumbled to the bed when Hickok passed out.

Josh expelled a long sigh, sleeving sweat off his forehead. He walked over to the washstand and rinsed the blood off his hands. Then he picked up Bill's gun, pulled a chair next to the bed, and settled in for a long stint of guard duty.

Chapter Fourteen

Two days after Josh's crude surgery, Wild Bill could easily sit up in bed and walk short distances. The two men played nickel-ante poker to wile away the time until Bill could ride again.

Following Bill's instructions, Josh whipped together a foul-smelling but healthful tonic of sulfur, black-strap molasses, and egg yolks. Bill, holding his nose, drank this restorative mixed with piping hot coffee to build up his depleted blood.

"I eavesdropped on the KP foreman at the cafe," Josh told Bill on the third day after the shootout at Ma Ketchum's. "They're going to need at least another two days to assemble a work crew."

137

Bill nodded, sorting out his discards. His neat mustache was growing back in. He wore only trousers and a long-sleeved cotton undershirt; but both Colt Peacemakers hung on the bedpost, only inches from his hands.

"I'm glad for the delay this time," Bill said. "Gives me time to get my fighting fettle back. I got a hunch I'll be needing it. Gimme three, kid."

Outside the hotel room, the setting sun was a dull orange disk balanced just above the western horizon. Two hours earlier, a special courier had arrived from Denver with the latest news from Pinkerton. Josh had read the letter aloud while Bill cleaned his fingernails with a match.

Although I've been disappointed at your progress so far, Pinkerton wrote, *your efforts have yielded some positive results after all, at least for the future. Thanks to your tip about the telegraph lines, we've assembled enough circumstantial evidence to intimidate a vice president of the Santa Fe Railroad.*

So far he has admitted to nothing. But he hints that he might be willing, in principle, to turn state's evidence against his coconspirators in exchange for immunity from criminal prosecution.

I expect that indictments will eventually be issued against several high officials of the SFRR. But the wheels of official justice turn very slowly out here on the frontier. No court action will happen soon enough to stop 'Bama Jones and Ansel

Logan. *Indictments will also be issued against those two, especially because of the slaughter of Captain Bledsoe and his men. But no one I've talked to believes Jones or Logan will ever be taken alive. Only gun law will "arrest" them.*

Despite this bit of good news, Jamie, I cannot emphasize enough how imperative it is to stop those two killers before they strike again. If they succeed one more time, the KP will abandon this project at a huge loss.

On a more personal note: A failure this important could perhaps cause irreparable damage to the Pinkerton Agency. If lawless thugs succeed in shaping America's destiny this time, they will be even bolder in future.

"That damned Pinkerton," Bill commented sarcastically when Josh finished reading, "ain't one to pressure a fellow, is he? Show your cards, kid. I got three tens with a king riding high."

But Josh noticed the brooding trouble in Bill's eyes. Pinkerton had indeed scraped a raw nerve.

"I'm saying he *could* be dead," Ansel Logan insisted. "I plugged him in the chest, not the arm."

"Plug a cat's tail," 'Bama shot back. "You call yourself a shootist, yet you brag on a chest hit? Shoo! A true marksman goes for the head every time. That's what you always tell me. Even a gut shot is better than a chest hit; it bleeds more. Hell, even my maw-maw knows that."

139

"To hell with your maw-maw, you damned ingrate! I kept Hickok and that city slick from shooting your fat ass while you escaped."

"So you did," 'Bama admitted, softening his tone. "So you did. A fine piece of work, bo. But I wish we coulda took our gear with us when we hightailed it."

The two hired killers had waited until nightfall before returning to Abilene to retrieve their saddles and rigging. Their horses were tethered in open grassland about a mile east of town. Now the two men stood in the shadow of the livery barn, carefully studying the town.

"If Hickok was dead," 'Bama pointed out, picking up that thread again, "there'd be a reg'lar fandango in the streets. It'd be a holiday hereabouts."

" 'At's true," Logan conceded. "Still . . . I'd wager Hickok is holed up in the Drover's Cottage, knitting his wound."

"Speaking of hotels," 'Bama said. "Where the hell *we* gunna stay? I'm damned if I want to hole up in Ellsworth again after what you done to that preacher's daughter, you sick son of a bitch."

Logan grinned, leaving his eyes out of it. "Ahh, she asked for it. Smilin' at me like she done. That gal wanted it bad. But never mind her."

Logan's tone changed as a new plan occurred to him. "Look . . . we need to hole up somewheres, right? Just for a few days, at most?"

"Didn't I just say so? Clean your damn ears."

"All right, then," Logan went on. "We need a safe place just until you can make one last kill. Then we can clear out of these parts. I know just the place. It'll be perfect."

'Bama studied his face in the buttery moonlight, finally taking Logan's point.

"Perfect for you, you mean. You're talking about that little blond gal's place."

"Perfect for *both* of us, porky. The McCoy girl's quarter section has got a crick out back with scrub trees bordering it. We can hide our horses in plenty of grass and water."

"That is handy," 'Bama had to admit. "Good location, too. We could see anybody approaching from miles off. Plus we can make that little heifer cook for us."

"Now you're whistling!"

Logan thumped the big man on his back. "Know what else?"

"What?" 'Bama said carefully, for he recognized his friend's reckless tone.

"I know the night clerk at the hotel. Wouldn't take but five dollars to find out what room Hickok's in."

"So what? I ain't looking to brace him," 'Bama protested.

"We won't. We'll just find out the room, then check things out from outside. There's a big empty lot out back. Way us two shoot? Why, hell! There's only the one story to the Drover's Cottage. If that room's got a window handy, we can easy

141

make it hot for Hickok and that weak sister who runs with him. We kill Hickok, fine. We don't?"

Logan shrugged. "Leastways we'll have a little fun before we leave town. And let that smug bastard know he ain't safe *no place* near us."

"The trick to knowing cards," Bill explained to Josh, "is to know people. 'Luck' is generally just the ability to recognize and seize an opportunity."

Bill nodded at the pile of nickels on the blanket beside him.

"I cleaned you out in less than two hours. But not because the cards have been falling my way. It's just that you can't bluff worth a kiss-my-ass, kid. Every time you have a bad hand, you chew on your lower lip. When you stop chewing, I cut my losses and fold. Gimme one, wouldja?"

Bill scooped up the card, his eyes slanting to the room's closed and curtained window.

"Think they'd come back to town?" Josh asked.

"Sure they would. Why not? I came back to this hole, didn't I? Kid, you're chewing up your lip again. I'm *trying* to make a cardplayer outta you."

"Hah! Tricked you that time," Josh gloated, slapping down his hand. "I've got a full house."

Bill flashed a grin. "Whips my pair of ladies. You're learning."

Hickok squinted as smoke curled up from the cheroot stuck between his teeth. Again Josh watched his gunmetal eyes cut toward the window.

"How you plan on stopping them next time?" Josh asked. "When the work crew goes back out, I mean?"

"I'll talk to the work-gang foreman tomorrow," Bill replied. "For starters, the workers will ride out in a coach car next time, not an open flatcar."

Josh shuffled the deck, then dealt himself and Bill five cards.

"Beyond that," Bill resumed, picking up his cards, "ain't a helluva lot I can do. I've scouted out the best ambush points. Long before the spike mauls start pounding, we'll be riding the danger line."

Bill fanned his cards open. Then Josh saw him frown so deeply that his reddish-blond eyebrows practically met.

"Oh, hell," Bill muttered. He stared at the two pairs in his hand.

Aces and eights.

His eyes flicked to the window again. And suddenly, Calamity Jane's recent words were snapping in Hickok's memory like burning twigs.

That old witch said beware the dead man's hand! Aces and eights will kill you, Bill!

"Kid," Bill said urgently, grimacing at the pain in his wound as he rolled off the bed, "hit the floor!"

Josh stared, his jaw dropping open. "But what—?"

Bill cursed and fetched Josh a hard kick to the hip even as Hickok tumbled. The moment Josh hit the floor, sheer bedlam was unleashed upon them.

The window glass exploded inward as a hammering racket of gunfire—rifle and pistol—shattered the calm night. Shards of glass sprayed a frightened Josh, and plaster dust spouted in white geysers as bullets pockmarked the wall behind them.

The lantern exploded, instantly starting a small fire; the porcelain wash bowl shattered; Bill's pillow coughed feathers as slugs ripped into it. Crawling below the hail of lead, Josh managed to smother the flames with a corner of blanket.

The volley lasted perhaps ten seconds. But it seemed an eternity to the two trapped men.

Finally, there was silence again except for the sound of frightened voices out in the hallway.

"You okay, kid?" Bill called out.

"I think so," Josh stammered. "Thanks to you, Wild Bill. How 'bout you?"

"Broke my damn scab open," Bill carped. "Wound's bleeding fresh. But no new holes, thank God."

Cautiously, both men sat up.

"How'd you know?" Josh demanded. "You hear something outside?"

Bill stared at his cards, now scattered on the floor faceup among broken glass. Somebody pounded on the door.

"Everything all right in there?" a nervous male voice demanded.

"Believe it or not, kid," Bill replied, "a curse can also be a blessing."

"That's too far north for me," Josh said, his face puzzled. "Whad'you mean?"

Again somebody thumped on the door. But Bill just stared again at the aces and eights scattered on the floor. Then he looked Josh straight in the eyes.

"I mean," Bill replied, "that Calamity Jane just saved our bacon again."

Chapter Fifteen

It was dawn, and a lovestruck Calamity Jane was as drunk as a poisoned coyote.

She heaved a tragic sigh, and it turned into a ghostly wraith in the cold morning air of early autumn.

Jane was too drunk to feel the cold, despite the fact that she wore only a threadbare pair of men's sailcloth trousers and a thin broadcloth shirt. She had lost her peg boots sometime during the night, as she wandered the prairie chanting Sioux war songs.

Once, her caterwauling had stampeded some cattle. But the night guards had recognized her and informed her she was too famous to shoot! Now empty Doyle's bottles littered the ground at her feet.

"Bill Hickok," she declared out loud, staring at her treasured portrait of the famous rogue. "You're as purty as a prince, and twice the man Sitting Bull ever was! But God shoot me straight to Hades if you ain't the cussedest man a gal could be fool' nuff to love!"

Jane meant to heave another sigh; instead, a whopping belch ripped from her, and the team almost spooked, thinking a bear was upon them.

Jane had a good campsite, picked according to her usual requirements: access to water, graze for the team, shelter from the wind, and good vision in all directions. Abilene, like most towns out west, had written a special public-nuisance ordinance forbidding Jane's presence within town limits after dark.

Towns, Jane figured, were just like Bill Hickok: They couldn't handle a real woman.

"To hell with all them pus-guts in town!" Jane informed the surrounding brake of dwarf oaks. "And all them blondes with the bouncy little titties, damn you, Wild Bill!"

Jane felt her head nodding. She decided to crawl in the back of her wagon and grab some shut-eye. It had been too quiet for days now. But last night, Jane had heard a dog howl while she was peeing—any fool could tell you that sign always meant trouble on the morrow. Trouble for Bill, which also meant trouble for her.

Except, she reminded herself sleepily, the morrow was here. Tomorrow was now today.

147

Jane went through the trees to the open meadow beyond. She moved the bays to new grass and tethered them long again. She turned to return to camp. That's when she spotted something just past the middle distance.

Jane narrowed her eyes and looked until she was sure of what she saw: two men digging what appeared to be a rifle pit. She couldn't make out the men clearly. But she knew that long headland beyond them marked the edge of the Kansas-Pacific's new spur-line project.

For a moment, Jane recalled the killing she witnessed in the work camp.

"You dry-gulching sons of bitches," the sleepy woman said almost gently.

Despite her exhaustion, Calamity Jane dug some charred wood out of her campfire and sketched a crude map on a scrap of flockboard she found in her wagon. She used a heavy *X* to mark the rifle pit.

Jane wanted sleep worse than they wanted ice water in hell. But her pretty Bill was in danger, and every instinct in her made that a priority like breathing.

Instead of going to bed, Jane untethered one of the bays and let it drink from a nearby rill. Then, riding bareback and hanging on with her knees, she headed into Abilene to give Bill her map.

Kristen was dropping dumplings into a pot of simmering beans when she heard footsteps out front of the soddy.

"Cameron!" she scolded without turning around. "I want you and your sisters to wash up *before* you come in! I set a bucket and a lump of soap near the door."

" 'Preciate that, sis. 'Preciate it all to hell."

It was a man's voice that answered. The shock of hearing it made Kristen gasp even before she turned around, fear icing her blood.

"It's gonna be good between me and you," promised the snake-eyed bully with a chewed twig in his mouth. "Oh, you'll scream out and claw my back. Girl, I'll make you see God before I climb off you! Hell, I might hafta go at it three, four times before I even lose my—"

"*Shut* your filthy whoremonger mouth!" 'Bama roared out. He was indifferent to the woman and would kill her in an eye blink, but carnal matters disturbed him, for he had a strict religious upbringing.

Ansel laughed, still staring at the terrified woman.

"You'll have to forgive ol' 'Bama here," he said. "See, his ma always made him sleep with his hands outside the blankets."

'Bama flushed a deep pink, and Logan laughed even harder.

"You said my name, you stupid bastard," 'Bama complained. "Right in front of her."

"It don't matter, porky. She ain't gonna repeat it, if you take my drift."

'Bama nodded at that. "But push the rut need

149

outta your thoughts for now," he snapped. "You can take care of that filth later if you gotta. Right now, you fool, we got to hide our horses, then find them damn kids 'fore they run for help."

Cameron was leading his little sisters, Sarah and Emily, up from the creek where they had been playing pirate games all morning. Abruptly, he spotted two horses in front of the house.

The next moment he remembered who the big sorrel belonged to—that mean man who wanted to hurt his sister.

The same man Cameron had beaned with a rock.

"Cripes," the savvy little seven-year-old said. "He'll either kill or cowhide me."

Cameron pushed his sisters down until the tall prairie grass hid them.

"Kristen's in trouble," he told them solemnly. "Bad trouble, the worstest kind. But if we go back to the house, we can't help her. We got to stick together, y'unnerstan'? Just like Pa told us before he went to live in heaven with Ma. You hear me?"

Both little towhead girls were blinking back tears. But their brother's strong-jutting chin made them feel braver. They both nodded.

"All right," Cameron said. "Don't matter if you're girls cuz you're both McCoys. Tough, just like Kristen."

The youth sent another worried glance toward the low soddy.

"Here's what we're gonna do," he resumed. "It's only two miles to the Kunkles' farm if we go back and follow the creek. But you'll both have to run fast and keep up with bubby, y'unnerstan'?"

"Will those men hurt Kristen?" Sarah wailed.

"Shh! Maybe not if we hurry up."

"But Mr. Kunkle is an old man like Grandpa Jim," Emily protested.

"Don't you worry," Cameron assured her. "Kristen's got a friend in town who's lots younger than Mr. Kunkle. He'll know what to do. I'll borrow a horse from the Kunkles and go get him. Now c'mon, you two, or the bad men will catch us!"

"Jane was drunk as a skunk when she made it," Wild Bill told Josh, studying the crude map she'd delivered earlier. "But I scouted that area earlier on the day Logan shot me. I can find the spot, all right."

Bill looked at Josh, his eyes thoughtful.

"Kid, you talked to the work foreman this morning?"

Josh nodded. "Work resumes tomorrow morning."

"That might give us enough time," Bill mused.

"Time for what?"

But instead of answering that question, Bill asked another. "Can you handle another ride to

151

Ellsworth? I don't trust the telegraph here in Abilene."

Josh shrugged. "The ride's boring, but it's easy. There's a good road for the short-line stage. Is it another telegram for Pinkerton?"

"It's a telegram, but not for Pinkerton."

Wincing only slightly at the pain in his wound, Bill crossed to the highboy and picked up a stub of pencil and a sheet of hotel stationery.

"This one's going to Fort Riley. I know the officer in charge of the quartermaster stores. There's an evening mail train comes into Abilene every night from the fort. We might be in time for a delivery."

"A delivery of what?" Josh demanded.

"You'll see soon enough," Bill promised him. "Just make sure you don't waste any time. That telegram will have to reach the fort by noon, or we'll miss the mail train."

A sudden thumping on the door startled both men. Instantly, each of Bill's fists was curled around a Colt.

"Hey, mister?" shouted a child's desperate voice. "Mister, are you in there? Them two bad men got my sister! *Please* help her!"

Chapter Sixteen

After he got Cameron McCoy's story, Bill sent the kid back to the Kunkle place.

"Real quick, go search out an honest cowboy who wants to make ten bucks," Bill instructed Josh, handing him a half-eagle gold piece and the telegram message. "Send him to Ellsworth in your place. I'll be requiring your services this morning."

While Josh took care of this task, Bill went to the livery and retrieved their horses. Moving a bit slower than usual, he rigged both horses and led them back to the hotel.

Bill observed that the reward notices had been torn down. Josh said locals had done it. Word was out that Wild Bill was here to stop the railroad assassins. Not everyone in this town was lawless—now Bill's enemies had to work more secretly.

Josh was waiting for him in the room.

"How can just the two of us do anything?" the reporter demanded. "That house sits wide open. It's the same problem we had before. How do you close in on shooters as good as those two? We need a posse, Bill."

"Don't matter what we *need,* kid. All that counts is what we got—just me and you. The sheriff of this rat hole is still down in Newton on 'court business.' The deputy he left is a bank robber I sent to prison three years ago. As for a posse— how in Sam Hill do I keep one of 'em from back-shooting me for the reward?"

Bill tossed his Winchester repeater onto the bed. "*You're* going to be our posse, Longfellow. Ever used one of these?"

Josh shook his head.

"Don't matter," Bill assured him. "I don't use it much, either, since my stagecoach days. But that's the rifle that won the West. You won't really need to hit anything. You just need to shoot it plenty—bust caps like a full-bore fool, I'm saying. Round after round until the barrel glows. Here, take this money and hustle over to the gun-shop. Pick up two one hundred-count boxes of .44 shells."

"But what—"

"Look, kid, it ain't no time for a newspaper inter-view! The McCoy girl might be dead already—or worse. Just get those damn shells, wouldja? I'll tell you more while we get closer to the house."

Keeping a long, low hill between them and the drab soddy, Bill and Josh rode in as close as they dared. It was midmorning by now, and the position of the sun, Bill explained to Josh, was critical.

"We're going to take a page from 'Bama's own book," Hickok said. "You'll be shooting out of the sun, which'll make it hard for 'Bama to draw a bead."

Both men had knelt in the thigh-high grass just below the crest of the low hill. The soddy was perhaps a thousand yards away.

"Set up ammo stations about ten yards apart," Bill instructed the nervous reporter. "Divvy up the shells into equal piles so they'll be all ready to load. Stay low and *stay in motion,* that's the main mile."

Bill gripped the kid's skinny arm and squeezed it hard to emphasize this last point.

"The moment you finish snapping off a few fast rounds from one station, hustle your butt to another. You stay in one spot too long, I guarantee: 'Bama Jones will swat you off this earth like a fly."

"I'll do it just like you say," Josh promised. "But I can't hit anything much from here."

"Yes, you can, you can pepper the front of the house so they think a posse is out here. The point is just to keep them distracted while I come up

155

through the grass behind the house. If you see a human shape inside, don't shoot at it—might be the girl."

Josh nodded. As usual, he was scared but also determined to do his part no matter what. Bill admired that trait in a man—the same dogged determination that had finally allowed northern clerks and farmers to win the war against the South's superior marksmen and horsemen.

"Just remember," Bill repeated, "stay low and keep moving."

Josh swallowed the fear lump in his throat.

"I will," he promised. "But you got the hard part, as usual. God almighty, Wild Bill! Don't let that Ansel Logan get the drop on you. He ain't no man—he's a killing machine."

Bill managed a nervy little grin. "I thank you for that word of encouragement. But that same appellation has been applied to me, also."

Josh flushed. He had forgotten calling Bill a "killing machine" once himself.

Bill said, "Give me about a twenty minute lead, hear? Then I want you to raise holy hell with that Winchester."

"We've looked all over the damn county," 'Bama complained as the two men returned to the soddy. "T'hell with them kids! By now they've gone for help. We got no choice but to clear out."

Logan banged open the split-slab door and stared at Kristen. She was tied up to a chair beside a low bed with a shuck mattress.

"But first," Ansel said, the tip of his tongue brushing his weather-cracked lips, "I got me a little business with sweet britches here. Why'n't you take a little walk, 'Bama?"

"Your brain gone soft? Didn't you hear me? Them brats foxed us; we got to git!"

"I said take a walk, you blue-nosed cracker! I got time for a quick poke. Either you light out, or you're gonna learn something useful, porky."

Before 'Bama could finish cursing, a quick *whump* sound in the sod wall out front was followed by the sharp crack of a rifle.

Several more shots, a brief pause, then another rifleman opened up on another section of the house.

Both men had crouched down at the initial burst of firing.

"Sounds like at least two men," 'Bama said.

"At least three," Logan corrected him a few moments later. A gunner had opened fire from a third position.

One of the rounds penetrated the sod and whanged off the cook stove, making 'Bama do a little jupe step.

"Christ!" he said, his voice higher from anxiety. "Somebody got up a posse!"

But Logan didn't seem so convinced.

"Sounds that way, don't it?" he said.

He cocked his head, listening as the shooting started again from the first position.

"Just answer me this," Logan said, stealing over near the door and peeking cautiously outside. "How's come we never hear the firing from more than one position at once?"

'Bama relaxed a bit when Logan's point sank home.

"Maybe," 'Bama replied, "on account it's a trick, that's how's come. What you'd call a diversion."

Looking more confident now, 'Bama picked up his Big Fifty from the table. "Think maybe I'll see if I can drop crosshairs on this 'posse.' "

Logan nodded, drawing his big Smith & Wesson. He dropped low.

"Kick this door shut quick behind me after I'm gone," he told his companion. "I'm taking a look outside."

Many people had expressed shock and disbelief when George "Iron Butt" Custer led his regiment to slaughter. But Wild Bill Hickok had not been at all surprised.

Hickok knew firsthand that Custer was the kind of man who went puny just before any combat engagement. Bill once observed Custer under pressure during the Civil War—as Jeb Stuart's cavalry attacked Custer's Michigan Wolverines, Custer had begun nervously repeating the same commands over and over until Bill told him to shut up. Bill figured that's why Custer always charged—it was the simplest, least complicated thing to do and required little thinking.

In sharp contrast, Wild Bill had been blessed with the lifelong ability to calmly separate himself from any situation—to be both participant and observer in the same moment. This trait kept him calm and rational when fear incapacitated other men.

Nonetheless, fear licked at his belly now as he moved through the tall grass about fifty yards north of the soddy. This was the toughest case Hickok had ever taken on for Pinkerton, and these two adversaries were unmatched in the black art of killing.

He moved forward mostly on his elbows and knees, trying to time his movements with the wind, so swaying grass wouldn't give him away. Bill wasn't too nervous, though, to appreciate the kid's shooting—Josh was following his instructions to the letter. And so far, nobody was shooting back from the soddy.

A moment later Bill cursed himself for failing to knock on wood—'Bama's powerful Sharps blasted, the noise so explosive Bill felt it more than heard it.

Silence from Josh's position.

Bill cast a nervous glance toward the sun. Had it shifted that much already, giving 'Bama a good line of sight?

"C'mon, kid," Bill urged under his breath when the silence stretched on. "You wouldn't let him hit you *that* easy."

Moments later Hickok expelled a relieved breath when Josh opened fire again.

Bill was dangerously close to one front corner of the soddy now. The wind gusted for a moment, bending the grass low out ahead of him, and Bill thought he might have glimpsed something up there. But the grass shifted back again before he could seize the image.

Just a dirt mound, Hickok decided. But some instinct deeper in him than thought made him lie stone still, a Colt ready to hand.

"Aww, this is sweet!" reported a man's voice from the house. "Logan, this is *sweet*, pard! I got a bead on the shooter—and guess what? It's that pup that trails Hickok. You hear me, Logan? He's going under, bo."

"*Shut* your goddamn mouth," Logan hissed, and Bill gave a violent start—the man was only a few feet in front of him in that tall grass!

But Bill could not seize the opportunity, not if he wanted to save Josh. The kid had gotten careless, and now was only moments away from death. There was no question of 'Bama Jones missing at this range.

Even as he stood up, Bill sent two quick rounds into the grass ahead of him, hearing Logan curse. Then the frontiersman spun toward the front door, hoping to drill 'Bama.

Unfortunately, it was a bad angle. All Bill could glimpse was the muzzle of the Big Fifty. He had to settle for spraying his remaining four rounds into the doorway.

Bill had the satisfaction of seeing the door fly shut. He had saved Josh that time. But the kid was on his own now—Bill had to save his own hide.

As Bill dropped down into the grass again, Logan opened fire.

Bullets whined past Bill, and despite the flaring pain in his wound he rolled hard and fast to get away. He got his left-side gun out of the holster while he rolled. He returned three rounds, but it was like trying to target shoot in dense fog.

But this blind shooting had unnerved Logan. He was up and running toward the house. Bill rose to his knees to plug him, but the deft circus shooter fired over his shoulder with amazing accuracy. Bill was forced to cover down again.

Now Bill was at a definite disadvantage. His enemies were sheltered inside with a good idea of his general location. Josh, no doubt running low on shells by now, had slowed his rate of fire. Hickok was essentially trapped on his own—any movement now to retreat would sign his death warrant.

Knowing what was surely coming, Bill willed himself calm and quickly reloaded. Moments later, the world seemed to explode around him.

'Bama and Logan tossed a deadly hail of lead into his position from the side window. Rounds thumped into the ground inches from him and one even nicked his left boot sole.

Bill dared not return fire until the men paused to reload. Then he hurled three shots through the window, rolling immediately to a new position under cover of his barrage.

That maneuver left Bill safe for the moment. The two killers had lost his location in the waving grass. But there was nothing Bill could hope to do now that they were alerted to his presence out there. He had lost the crucial element of surprise.

Josh had finally ceased firing, and Bill knew he must be out of ammo. Minutes ticked by, seeming like hours. Hickok was still debating his next play when Logan's voice rang out from the house.

"Hickok? You hear me?"

But Bill knew better than to answer and reveal his position.

"Hickok, lissenup! I got my gun on your little sweetheart's head right now, you savvy? 'Bama is going to leave the house and go back toward the creek. You *will not* shoot him, you got that, big man? Try anything, and I'll paper the walls with this whore's brains!"

Raising his head only a few inches, Bill watched in stomach-tightening frustration while 'Bama Jones scuttled outside and hustled back toward the creek. Then Bill heard hooves escaping to the west.

"Hickok! You done real good, gunman, following my orders! Now lissenup again. I'm coming out next, and I'll have the woman in front of me. Try anything cute, and I'll plug the bitch. You got that, big man?"

Bill rolled onto his uninjured side to ease the throbbing pain. He could feel blood trickling down his side where he'd torn the scab open again. He spat grass out of his mouth and thumbed back the hammer of his Peacemaker.

"Yeah, I got it, Logan," he whispered in the sawing grass. Then Hickok, calm and steady now, waited for the door to open.

Chapter Seventeen

Wild Bill heard the door ease open slowly. He kept his head low in the grass, knowing he couldn't give a shooter like Ansel Logan even the slightest target.

But Logan obviously had the same respect for Hickok. Bill could hear him giving terse orders to Kristen McCoy.

"You don't move one inch, sugar britches, without my say-so, got it? You make even a twitch, I'll blow you to kingdom come."

Bill parted some grass just enough to glimpse them as they came around the corner of the house. Logan, who was short anyway, hunched even lower to keep the girl in front of him. He moved with exaggerated slowness and care, afraid to give Hickok even a moment's target.

164

"You're doing real good, sweet love," Logan encouraged her.

"Go to hell, you pig," she shot back. Raising her voice, she called; "Mister Hickok? I'm doing what this piece of garbage tells me to do because I've got a family to care for. But you have my blessing to shoot me if it means stopping this murderer."

Logan laughed at that. " 'At's real noble, darlin'. Real brave and pure. Sends shivers right up my spine. But ol' Mister Hickok won't shoot no woman. He's a *gallant* man, you see. Got him a code of chivalry like them knights under King Arthur, see?"

The couple moved slowly along the east side of the soddy now. Desperately, Bill stared through the grass and watched for the slightest opportunity. But Logan, of all people, knew about the vulnerabilities of the human body. Expertly, he kept Kristen in front of his vital spots at every moment.

Bill calculated the possibilities quickly. Logan was giving him an occasional clear shot at a foot or ankle, now and then an arm or elbow.

But a wound would not keep Logan from reflexively twitching his trigger, killing Kristen.

He might kill her anyway, Bill thought. Even if he gets clear of me. But Hickok wouldn't play God with that decision. Logan was right about one thing: Men could say what they liked about Bill Hickok, but he did indeed follow a code. And one key tenet of that code was *always defend the defenseless*.

"Yeah, noble Hickok," Logan taunted, still inching his way alongside the house to safety. "He don't *take* his women; they surrender to him willingly. Ain't that sweet and lovely?"

Bill knew Logan was trying to taunt him into speaking so he could find a target. Logan was also mouthing off just to cover his own fear. Besides the scorn and hatred in his voice, Bill also detected a frightened man.

If only, Bill told himself in frustration, Logan would just expose his head. How often had Ansel Logan reiterated his theme about a head shot being the only guaranteed one-bullet kill with a pistol?

Now and then Wild Bill got a tantalizing glimpse as the top of Logan's head bobbed into view for a moment. But the trick shooter took great pains to stay hunkered down behind Kristen.

They were beyond the house now, moving inexorably closer to the creek and Logan's waiting horse. Bill knew he was losing the opportunity. Another minute or so, and Logan would be at an impossible angle unless Hickok moved to a new position—which could well prove fatal.

"Bill?" Kristen called out, surprising both men.

"Shut your damn mouth!" Logan ordered tersely.

"I want to say good-bye to Bill, you pig," Kristen said hotly. "What are you going to do about it, kill me?"

"I said shut your gob, bitch!"

"Bill?" Kristen went on bravely. "I really *fell* for you in a big way, know that?"

"Put a sock in it, whore!" Logan raged. "Nobody gives a damn about your sweet nothings."

But Bill felt elated blood humming in his veins, and he primed himself to make his move. Logan, in his nervousness, missed it. But Kristen had a perfect grasp of this situation—and she had just signaled to Bill to get ready to seize the opportunity.

A few steps later, Kristen made her dangerous move.

As she had just hinted, she abruptly *fell*—just went limp and dropped straight down, opening up a target for Wild Bill.

Logan snarled with rage, but knew better than to worry about shooting the rebellious bitch now. He dove for cover himself—but in midleap, a slug from Wild Bill's Peacemaker punched into his skull, and the former star of Buffalo Bill's Wild West Show was dead before he hit the ground.

Kristen, who had been strong for so long, now gave vent to tears of relief in Wild Bill's arms. Bill assured her the kids were safe at the Kunkles. But his mind was really on 'Bama Jones and that rifle pit.

Bill crossed his fingers, hoping his telegram got through to Fort Riley and that there'd be a delivery for him on the mail train tonight.

* * *

167

'Bama waited for six hours at the rendezvous point he and Logan had established along the Wyandott River. When his partner failed to show, the sniper reluctantly concluded the obvious: Hickok had managed to kill him.

Without Ansel Logan as his bodyguard, 'Bama felt naked and exposed. But now this job was almost over. One more kill, and the KP would abandon this spur line. In that event, 'Bama stood to earn a huge bonus.

It was worth the risk, he decided. Especially since the new rifle pit was in an excellent location to defend himself. 'Bama decided to drop one surveyor or worker, then simply hightail it into the southwest country. He could collect his bonus in Santa Fe, then follow the Rio Grande down into Old Mexico.

He spent a fitful night in a cold camp beside the river, gnawing on jerked buffalo meat. Just past dawn, he hobbled his horse in a patch of black-jack near the rifle pit.

Pockets of mist still hung out over the KP tracks. 'Bama made a careful study of the entire area. Nobody was at work yet, but it wouldn't be long now. A typical workday out west still went from sunup to sundown. No sign of Hickok, either.

'Bama crouched at the edge of the pit and slid his Big Fifty out of its buckskin sheath. With loving care, he screwed the metal bipod onto an attachment below the flash suppressor. Then he checked his windage and elevation knobs, making sure they were set for the proper range.

One last shot. One little tickle of the trigger. And then he could flee this area forever, a rich man for the rest of his days. Not that he was ready to give up sniping—'Bama had killed this way for so long that it had become a way of life with him, something more than just a job. He found *meaning* in it, too.

'Bama felt a queer sensation just before he jumped into the rifle pit—a sudden conviction that he shouldn't jump in at all.

He glanced inside, but nothing was wrong.

"Goddamn you, Hickok," he said out loud. "You're giving me the fidgets."

'Bama leaped inside, landed in the soft dirt, suddenly heard a faint fizzling sound that seemed vaguely familiar from his war days.

And then he remembered: That fizzling noise was the detonator powder in a shrapnel-filled device known as the Adam's Pressure Mine.

"NO!"

The big man made one desperate attempt to claw his way out of the pit. Instead, he was blown out—in a bloody spray of a detached leg and exposed intestines. Unlike Logan's, his death was slower and more agonizing—and he had time to curse the carrion birds that began gathering for the feast.

* * *

"Fire in the hole!" Wild Bill sang out triumphantly when 'Bama Jones came hurling out of the rifle pit.

Bill handed the field glasses to Josh. The young reporter took one brief look at the bloody mess writhing beside the pit, then handed the glasses back to Bill.

"Like Jane said about Wilson," Josh remarked. "Looks like he's past a poultice."

Bill nodded, slipping the glasses back into his saddle bag.

"This spur line will go through after all," Bill said. "But if that Adam's Mine hadn't come in last night, I woulda been forced to hide in that shallow pit. And pray God 'Bama didn't spot me while he was coming in."

"Where to now?" Josh asked. "Back to Denver?"

Bill nodded, slipping the glasses back into his saddle bag.

"Might's well ride," he said. "We could book passage on the train. But it's a straight shot west from here."

But Josh noticed Bill was gazing toward the northeast—the direction of Kristen McCoy's place. And a little smile was tugging at his lips. Bill had not returned to the hotel after planting the mine last night. And Josh discreetly asked no questions.

"But first," Bill suggested, grabbing his saddle horn and stepping up and over, "why'n't we ride past the McCoy place one last time, see how they're doing?"

However, the two men had just set out when a familiar buckboard abruptly appeared on a low ridge out ahead of them—as if to deliberately cut them off in that direction.

Bill cussed, but without heat. He met Josh's mirthful eyes. Bill suddenly laughed out loud and wheeled his horse around toward the west again.

"God kiss me! Someday I'm going to *shoot* that damn woman," Bill vowed. "But I confess that right now she still scares the living hell outta me. C'mon, Longfellow, case closed. Let's dust our hocks toward Denver!"

KIT CARSON

BLOOD RENDEZVOUS
DOUG HAWKINS

The high point of any trapper's year is the summer rendezvous, the annual gathering where mountain men from all over the frontier meet to trade the pelts they risked their lives for. But for Kit Carson, the real danger lies in getting to the rendezvous. He is leading a party of trappers, all of them weighed down with a year's worth of furs. That is enough to make them a tempting target for any killer on the trail—especially when the trail leads through Blackfoot territory.

_4499-4 $3.99 US/$4.99 CAN

Dorchester Publishing Co., Inc.
P.O. Box 6640
Wayne, PA 19087-8640

Please add $1.75 for shipping and handling for the first book and $.50 for each book thereafter. NY, NYC, and PA residents, please add appropriate sales tax. No cash, stamps, or C.O.D.s. All orders shipped within 6 weeks via postal service book rate. Canadian orders require $2.00 extra postage and must be paid in U.S. dollars through a U.S. banking facility.

Name_____
Address_____
City_____State_____Zip_____
I have enclosed $_____ in payment for the checked book(s).
Payment <u>must</u> accompany all orders. ❑ Please send a free catalog.
    CHECK OUT OUR WEBSITE! www.dorchesterpub.com

KIT CARSON

COMANCHE RECKONING

DOUG HAWKINS

There is probably no better tracker in the West than the famous Kit Carson. With his legendary ability to read sign, it is said he can track a mouse over smooth rock. So Kit doesn't expect any trouble when he sets out on the trail of a common thief. But he hasn't counted on a fierce blizzard that seems determined to freeze his bones. Or on a band of furious Comanches led by an old enemy of Kit's—an enemy dead set on revenge.

___4453-6 $3.99 US/$4.99 CAN

KIT CARSON

The frontier adventures of a true American legend.

#2: Ghosts of Lodore. When Kit finds himself hurtling down the Green River into an impossibly high canyon, his first worry is to find a way out—until he comes face-to-face with a primitive Indian tribe preparing for a battle in which, one way or another, he will have to take sides.

___4325-4 $3.99 US/$4.99 CAN

#1: The Colonel's Daughter. Kit Carson's courage and strength as an Indian fighter have earned him respect throughout the West. And when the daughter of a Missouri colonel is kidnapped, Kit is determined to find her—even if he has to risk his life to do it!

___4295-9 $3.99 US/$4.99 CAN